CW00519949

WILD AND FREE

Sanctuary Book1

By
Michelle Dups

<u>DEDICATIONS</u>

This book is dedicated to my Ouma. Because of you, I started my love affair with romance books when you introduced me to them as a teenager. You are the rock that holds our family together and I hope you will be with us for many more years. Even though we now live on different continents you are never far from my thoughts. This one is for you!

WILD AND FREE

Sanctuary Book1

Chapter 1

DEX

MacGregor Hills Ranch

I looked at my younger brother in frustration. "What do you mean we need to hire another vet?"

"It would seem that Shelly got tired of living out in the boonies," replied Jett. "On the last trip to the city when we went for supplies, she decided to stay. Apparently, she met someone at the hotel bar and that was it."

Zane watched as I scrubbed my face with my hands in frustration and look up at the ceiling.

"So, what the fuck do we do now?" I asked the two of them.

"We can always have Reggie come and cover," suggested Jett.

"Reggie, Reggie, do I know Reggie?" I asked.

"Doubtful," Jett replied. "We went to school together in the States. Reggie started off in medicine but didn't enjoy it so changed to veterinary."

"Okay," I said.

"If this Reggie is happy to move to the boonies with the nearest town four hours away, and for the pay and board we offer, have him start as soon as possible"

"Ah, Reggie isn't…." Jett began while in the corner of his eye he saw Zane shaking his head.

"I'm sure Reggie will be happy to start as soon as possible," Zane said with a smirk.

I looked at Zane suspiciously, "Is there something I need to know about Reggie?"

Both of my brothers looked at me and slowly shook their heads. "No, nothing that I can think of," said Zane.

"Do we need to hide what we are?" I asked.

"No, Reggie is a wolf so no need to hide," said Jett.

"Thank fuck for that. At least that's one less thing to worry about. Okay, Jett, I'm leaving it up to you to get the paperwork sorted and get Reggie out here ASAP. Let me know if you need anything more from me."

I stood up.

"I'm heading out to the hot springs for a dip. This has been a shit week, what with the poachers, cattle getting stuck in the mud, and now having to arrange a new vet."

"I'll see you guys later. Have Maggie put a plate aside for me, please?"

I left out the side door of the library and took in the beautiful orange sunset as it slowly faded away into the sky. I could smell rain in the air and hoped that we got some soon. The rivers and dams were slowly drying out, which meant the poachers were out in full force trying to get enough food to feed their families.

I shook myself and stepped out of my clothes. I put them in the basket on the veranda that was left there just for this purpose.

The change come over me. My eyesight became clearer, my hearing better. My leopard made a chuffing noise, happy to be out as I bounded off the veranda. I marked a few trees with my claws as I made my way. The breeze felt so good as it ruffled my fur, and my leopard was happy to stretch out, as I ran toward the natural hot springs about a kilometre away. Still, in my leopard form, I made my way slowly into the hot springs. My stress melted away as I turned back into my human form. Laying my head back on the rock behind me, I looked up at the stars in the night sky. I was tired. Surely it was wrong to feel so worn down by the age of thirty-three. I had taken on the care of my younger brothers and the ranch after my parents died when I was nineteen. At the time, Falcon had been seventeen, Jett sixteen, Duke fourteen, and Zane thirteen. It had been hard, but we'd done it, and made the ranch even more of a success. We were almost completely self-sufficient now. As I lay there looking at the stars, I realised I was lonely. Sure, I could go into town on the next supply run for some company, but I wasn't feeling it anymore.

Still, there was no use sitting and moping. I got out of the pool and stood in the dark drying off, listening to the sounds of the frogs and crickets. I watched the bats swooping down and heard the lowing of the cattle in the distance. After changing back into my leopard, I slowly made my way home to my brothers. As I got closer, I heard them laughing and joking around.

For a while, I stood and looked at the home my great-great-grandfather had built for my great-great-grandmother. Back then, it only had three-rooms, then as the family grew, it grew with them. With each child they had added a room, and each bedroom had a door to the veranda that could be left open in the hot months. All in all, there were now a total of twelve bedrooms. Two years ago, I had upgraded them and, where I could, added bathrooms so that some were self-contained.

The outside of the house and the veranda columns were white. The concrete floor was smooth from all the feet that had walked on it. And the floor of the veranda was a beautiful green, polished to a high shine. Big pots of beautiful elephant ear plants, ferns and begonias were scattered around. In summer, it was great to sit and relax here. So beautiful to look at and so cool in the heat of the day.

I walked inside to grab a shower. After my shower I went to the kitchen to pick up the supper plate Maggie had put aside for me and joined Falcon in the family room.

"Where are the others?" I asked.

"Either headed to bed or gone out for a run," Falcon answered. He turned from away from his book and looked at me his eyebrow raised.

"So, I hear I'm getting a new vet?" Falcon said.

"So, it seems," I replied. "Try not to run this one off, yeah?" I grinned.

"You fucker," he laughed. "I didn't run the last one off. You showed no interest in her when she was panting after you, so she found someone else," he grinned.

"What?" I asked. "I didn't even say two words to the woman." I shook my head. "Well, at least we don't have to worry about that with the next one as it's a bloke."

Falcon choked on his beer.

"What?" I questioned. "Am I missing something about Reggie?"

"Not as far as I know," replied Falcon. "I know that Reggie was top in the graduating class and has a couple of years' experience. Went to college on scholarships and was brought up in foster care by a couple of bears."

"I thought wolves looked after their own."

"Usually," responded Falcon, "But it seems Reggie's parents were part of a mixed pack, so when they died in a flood in Louisiana, Reggie went through state-sponsored human foster care, and eventually ended up with a Bear Shifter family that had been old friends of

Reggie's mum. Sadly, Reggie was just one of many they fostered."

I nodded. "Okay, as long as you're happy, as he'll be spending most of his time with you. I'm heading to bed." I finished my beer, dropped my plate off in the kitchen, and went to bed.

Chapter 2

REGGIE

As I watched from the small window, the four-seater plane I was in did a circle around the property owned by the Macgregor Brothers. The ranch was vast. Nearly twenty thousand acres, mostly used for Grade A beef, and the crops they grew to feed the cattle. They ran horses that were used for running the ranch, and a few pigs and goats that seemed to be mostly for food for the MacGregors and their staff.

"Nearly there now," stated the pilot who had introduced himself as John when he collected me from the main airport in the capital this morning. "I'm going to do a quick flyover of the house, so they know to make their way to the airstrip."

Nodding, I gave him a thumbs-up sign. My wolf was not a happy bunny and was itching to get out after being stuck in aeroplanes for the last two days. I hadn't had anywhere safe to shift, and I was about ready to tear my own skin off.

I hoped it was Jett that was collecting me as he'd understand what I needed without me having to explain. I smiled when I thought of my friend, or I thought I did. The pilot was giving me a strange side-eye look, so I guess my trying to keep a lid on the rumbling from my wolf wasn't working.

"Upset stomach," I grimaced.

"Ah," he nodded looking sympathetic. "Looks like they are ready for you." He pointed at a Land Rover parked by the side of a runway.

Looking at the two people standing by the vehicle. I realised with relief that one was Jett. The other must be one of his brothers going by the same shade of auburn hair.

The plane hadn't fully stopped when I was ripping my seatbelt off, and impatiently waiting for the door to be opened. I rushed down the steps straight for Jett. He took one look at my face and grabbed me in a tight hug.

"Go out to the trees and change, I'll get your stuff."

I took off without even a 'thank you' to the pilot.

"Wow, she must need to go, huh," I heard the pilot say. "Her stomach's been growling for the last forty-five minutes."

Jett raised an eyebrow and laughed at John's comment. They'd been using John's piloting services for years. "She'll be fine. She's a tough cookie."

"How have you been, John?" Zane asked as they shook hands.

John was in his late sixties and the brothers kept expecting him to retire soon, but like he always said, *'not until I'm in a pine box'.*

"Can't complain, Zane," he replied as he nodded at them both.

"How are things out here on the ranch? Are you ready to unload? Maggie ordered a shit load of flour and such for you guys. Plus, the little lady that just went into the bush has a ton of veterinary equipment and meds with her."

"Thanks, John. We have the lads arriving with another truck shortly. Maggie ordered more than usual, as the managers in the north and south areas of the ranch need stock as well," explained Zane.

"Reggie will be helping Falcon with the small animal care that's taking all his time if you don't mind putting the word out that there's a new vet at the MacGregor Ranch," Jett said, shielding his eyes from the sun with his hand.

"Can do, Jett. No worries." He turned towards the trees, "Here she comes."

I'd heard this entire conversation from the trees, where I'd shifted quickly to appease my wolf. Once she was done rolling around, stretching, and taking in her new environment, she settled. It wasn't often she made herself known, as she was pretty laid back, so I wasn't surprised to feel contentment come over her as I shifted back to human form and got dressed.

Making my way over to Jett and the others. I grinned, "Sorry about that. Feel much better now."

I hugged Jett hard. "How are you doing, my friend?" I looked up at him and smiled. "Missed your stupid face."

He grinned at me. "I missed your stupid face more."

A snort of laughter came from the tall man leaning against the Land Rover, and Jett rolled his eyes. "Reggie, this is my very little brother Zane, the accountant, but we try not to hold that against him."

Zane straightened up and moved toward us. Like his brother, he was tall, well over six-foot-four, with wide shoulders and a swagger. He threw me a charming grin and I thought, *'Hoy this one is trouble.'*

"Accountant, eh? You poor thing. Did they not have anything else for you to do?"

"Hey now, don't be dissing us, accountants. We can make bad things happen with just a flick of a button. A few zero's here, a couple of minuses there." He grinned at me, then reached out and pulled me into a hug. "Nice to meet you, Reggie."

"You too, you big oaf. I can't breathe."

"Oops, my bad," he said. "I forget my own strength sometimes."

I rolled my eyes at him. Just then another 4x4 pulled up. It was the ranch hands to load up all the stock we had brought.

"These are the Doc's," John said, bringing over my bags and the veterinary supplies. "I'm heading off now," He turned to me and shook my hand.

"It was lovely meeting you, Doc. Hopefully, I'll see you again and I hope you feel better soon."

"Thanks for getting me here safely, John. It was a pleasure to meet you too." I smiled at him.

Jett clapped his hands together. "Right," he said. "Let's get you up to the main house and settled in. Then we'll get you introduced to everyone."

"Yeah, can't wait for Dex to meet you," grinned Zane.

I looked at him suspiciously. "Why do you say it like that?"

Jett sighed. "Dex may be under the impression that you're male."

"Why the hell would he think that?"

"Because that's what he assumed, and we didn't clarify the matter. He left it up to us to sort out a new vet and you're the best I've ever worked with and I wanted you here. I worried that if he knew you were female, he'd veto it as head of the family. Unfortunately, we haven't had much luck with female vets," Jett explained.

Feeling a little frustrated, I looked at my long-time friend and I could see the worry in his eyes. "Well, what's done is done. He better not bloody fire me though. If he does, I'm taking it out of your hide, Jett, so be prepared."

"Ah, he won't fire you," Zane said, as he threw an arm around my shoulders with a grin. "We won't let him."

I pushed his arm off me. "You are trouble," I said. "Let's get to the house and face the music. Hopefully, you can feed me first before everything kicks off because I'm starving". I looked around me not seeing any kind of house.

"How far is it to the house, anyway?"

"About twenty minutes' drive," Jett said.

I got into the vehicle, and since there were only front seats, Zane jumped in the back. I wiped my forearm across my forehead. It was sweltering out in the sun. Must remember to always wear a hat when I'm outside. We sped along, past the yellow grass blowing in the breeze and I noted how dry the ground was.

"Is it always this dry?" I asked looking at Jett.

"No, you've hit us right at the height of the dry season. We only have two seasons here. Wet and dry. We'll hopefully be getting the first rains soon. It's the end of October now, and they usually start in November. We're praying it's a good rainy season, as we're having issues with the rivers and dams drying up. The dry season is our winter season and starts around April or May."

By now, we were moving up a tree-covered drive, the coolness of the shade a welcome contrast to the hot sun we had been driving in. What came into view was the most beautiful house I had ever seen. The vehicle ahead of us drove round to the back while we parked under a carport next to the front of the house.

"Wow, it's beautiful."

"It's home," said Zane, jumping out and landing almost soundlessly next to me. He gave me a hand out of the vehicle as if on autopilot.

"I can get out of a vehicle." I said grinning at him, even as I took his hand.

He seemed surprised to see my hand in his. "Sorry." He looked sheepish. "Habit. Dad always had us help Mum out of the vehicle."

"No worries. It's nice that you remembered." Going with instinct, I hugged him and smiled up at him.

From the veranda, I heard, "Zane, stop flirting with my vet, I need this one to stay."

Looking up, I saw a grinning man, and I could see straight away that it was another of the brothers. They all had the same muscular build with auburn hair, brown eyes and dimples.

The only way to tell them apart seemed to be by their facial hair.

I assumed that this grinning brother was Falcon, my immediate boss. I walked up to him and shook his hand.

"Hi, I'm Reggie, it's great to meet you. I've heard a lot about all of you from Jett when we were at school together."

Then, as seemed to be the custom among the MacGregor Brothers, I got pulled into a hug by Falcon. When the hug was done, he pushed me back and held me by my shoulders.

"Good to meet you, Reggie. I'm Falcon. I'm so happy to have you here, and I can't wait to show you around. How about we get you in, and show you to your room so you can freshen up? Then, we can have lunch and I'll give you a tour. Dex and Duke won't be back until this evening. They're at a meeting with the other families."

Nodding in agreement, I wondered what it was about these brothers that made me feel like I was home and safe. I hadn't had this feeling since my parents had passed away. As wonderful as my foster parents were, I didn't have the same feeling of family and home while living with them. Once I'd moved out to college, I just couldn't seem to settle anywhere.

"Sounds fantastic to me. I'm starving."

Chapter 3

DEX

Duke and I were travelling to a meeting of the four main families that lived in this block.

For two centuries our families had each been in charge of two hundred thousand acres that had been passed down from generation to generation. The original chief of the tribe was named Abioye, he had tasked our families to look after the people and the animals, to make sure they all continued to thrive.

Shifters had been around since the beginning of time and our families had originated in the United States. During the witch trials, they had had to flee as they had been outed as witches, entire clans were being killed by beheading.

Somehow our families had survived and made it to the coast.

At the time it was unusual for different shifter breeds to mix, they all met by coincidence on the same ship. All the families managed to secure passage to Europe and decided they should stick together for safety and pool their resources.

How they ended up in Africa is unclear, from stories handed down, we had been told that our ancestors had each sent a mated couple out into the world, the four couples had stuck together and ended up here. They had helped a group of villagers that were being attacked. Tribal warfare was rife during those times. One of the group, being attacked happened to be the young son of the chief. During the attack, they had changed into their animals to better aid the group. Instead of running in horror the chief's son had taken them home and explained to the chief what had happened.

The tribe had lore about shifters and a prophecy that four shifter families would be tasked with protecting the people of this region. The four mated couples had agreed and stayed.

The four main families consist of us the MacGregors, the Russos, the Landrys and the Moores.

The Russos are, Hyena Shifters. I know most other shifters are put off by Hyena Shifters, but the Russo family are fantastic hunters and loyal lifelong friends of ours.

Next come the Landry's they're Wild Dog Shifters and are fantastic in a crisis. They have a strong sense of family and are amazingly generous to all that know them. But you certainly don't want to piss them off; they'll turn vicious on a dime if need be.

The fourth family is the Moores, Elephant Shifters. This generation consists of four Amazonian females and their father. They're great women until riled, then you want to get out of their way. It's always interesting when we go out in the city with them.

Meetings are held in a building we'd built at the point where the four pieces of land meet. None of us wanted to travel to the city for meetings, so this is more convenient for all of us. We meet once a quarter unless there's an emergency.

This meeting was to discuss the increase in poaching that we'd been having. To see what, we could do about it.

Pulling in under the trees, I could see that the other families had already arrived and were sitting in the cool shade.

Duke and I got out and made our way over. It's usually just the firsts and the seconds of each family that met for these meetings.

We exchanged hugs and backslaps with Anton and Luca Russo, Joel and Amy Landry, and Renee and Lottie Moore.

"Beer?" asked Lottie, holding up two cold ones.

I didn't usually, but this time I grabbed one from her and took a long pull. It was hotter than hell at the moment and the cool brew soothed not just my throat but my leopard. He was not happy today and had been fighting me for control for the last couple of hours. I wasn't sure what was up with him and just wanted to get this meeting over with.

I turned to find them all looking at me, I wasn't usually one to drink alcohol, so they knew something was up.

"All good?" Duke queried.

"Not sure, my leopard is riding me hard today, and I'm not sure why."

Anton Russo cleared his throat. "Right, why don't we get started then, so you can get home and let him roam? Hopefully, that'll help."

I nodded at my friend. For all their size the Russo brothers were soft-hearted. Both of them were six foot and built of solid muscle, with tanned skinned and curly black hair. The only difference between them was that Luca's eyes were bright blue eyes while Anton's were dark.

The size difference between them and the Landrys was huge. Joel and Amy were both just under six foot, both were slim and wiry. They had brown eyes and brown hair with light streaks running through.

Renee and Lottie Moore were both six foot and well-muscled with long hair. All the Moore females had different coloured hair, but as they all had different mothers that wasn't surprising. Renee's hair was red, Lottie's dark brown almost bordering on black. Their twin sisters Ava and Marie had blonde hair, but all the Moore sisters had their father's green eyes.

"I agree," Renee said, "Let's get started."

Between the four families, we ran a couple of businesses together as well as our own concerns. Amy and Zane did all our accounts, so Zane joined us via a conference call to update us. We all seemed to be doing fine financially, which was great after a couple of tough years.

We decided to increase the patrols around the perimeters to see where the poachers were getting in. Hopefully, we could catch some and find out where they were selling their spoils.

I breathed a sigh of relief when the meeting finished, and we all got up to leave. It was clear they had all cut it short for my sake, and the way my leopard was pushing at me. My eyes were constantly changing, and my claws kept emerging.

"Right, I think that's enough. Dex needs to get home," I heard Joel say. "Do you want to maybe get the claws out of the table brother?" Joel grinned at me.

Looking down, I saw that I had clawed grooves into the table. I retracted them and ran my hands over my face. "I'm sorry, I'm not sure what's going on. The last time I felt like this …" I trailed off.

Duke looked at me grimly. "When the folks died."

"Yeah." I nodded.

"Why don't you call the boys and make sure all is okay?" suggested Lottie. I looked at Duke and nodded. He got out his phone and walked off.

I looked at the others around the table. "Sorry that we have to cut this short. Let me know if there's anything you need us to do."

"Don't worry about it," Lottie said, getting up and coming over to hug me. There was nothing behind her action. Lottie was a hugger and her hugs felt just like hugging a sibling.

"I hope everything's okay at home. Let us know." She I looked at me with worried eyes.

"I will," I said, kissing her forehead.

Duke came back in. "Falcon says they are all good. The new vets arrived, and they're going a ride around the property to familiarise the vet with everything. Falcon hasn't felt that anything's off, but he'll keep an eye out, and keep in touch."

I breathed a sigh of relief. At least they were all okay. We said our goodbyes to the others and left.

I looked at Duke. "You drive. I'm not in control enough."

"Do you need to go for a run before we leave? That may help."

"No, my leopard is pushing for us to keep moving. If I change, he may take off and I don't want to leave you to travel back by yourself with all that's going on."

He nodded. Getting in the Land Rover, Duke took the wheel and we off for home.

Chapter 4

REGGIE

Falcon showed me to my room. It was huge with a full ensuite bathroom, king-size bed, chest of drawers and wardrobe.

"Wow, this is gorgeous. I've never had a room this nice."

"Dex had all the bedrooms redone and added on the ensuite last year. Sometimes we have people stay over and it's easier if they have their own bathroom," Falcon explained.

"The doors open onto the inside veranda, and it's safe to open the doors to let the breeze in, but just make sure you have the mosquito net down or you'll be eaten alive."

I looked at him. "Falcon, I can't thank you enough for taking me on. Since college, I've kind of been coasting, so I'm looking forward to getting stuck into this job. Let me freshen up and I'll be ready to have a look round."

"After you feed me, of course!" I grinned at him.

He laughed. "You definitely won't be hungry for long. Maggie puts on a huge lunch. Come down to the dining room when you're done. Will you be able to find it?"

I tapped my nose. "Wolf, remember?" I said with a grin.

He grinned back, tapped the door jam and left me to it.

I unpacked quickly, looking for a fresh set of clothes that were more suitable for the weather. Khaki shorts and a turquoise tank top sounded good, paired with hiking boots. I also found my hat, in case we were out in the sun.

Going into the bathroom, I started the shower, and while that warmed up, I looked at myself in the mirror. My long, curly, blonde hair needed a good wash. I studied my face and marvelled that not once had anyone said anything about my eyes, which made for a nice change. I had been born with one green and one blue eye, which someone always had to comment on.

The rest of me was unremarkable, I thought. Pretty short for a shifter at five foot six, with a decent enough body thanks to my shifter genes. I wouldn't have minded having a bit more bust and butt, like my sister April, but unfortunately, that part of me seemed to have stopped when I hit fourteen.

Shrugging, I got in the shower. No use wishing, because if wishes were horses, I'd have a herd, I could hear my foster mother say.

I felt ten times better after a shower, and probably smelt better too. The boys had been kind enough not to say anything, but I'm sure they smelt me from a mile away.

While I got dressed, I left my hair down to dry out and put a hair tie on my wrist, because I knew having it down would eventually drive me crazy. It reached down to my butt and there was plenty of it. As I left my room, a breeze blew through the windows, bringing with it the most amazing citrusy smell. Instead of turning left to the dining room I turned right to follow the smell. My wolf was now pushing at me. This was a surprise as she very rarely made herself known. I think she's the most laid-back wolf out there. The closer I came to the double doors at the end of the corridor the stronger it became. Pressing myself up against them, I inhaled deeply, feeling my eyes roll to the back of my head. With a moan I pushed open the doors. My wolf was going crazy. All I could think was *"mine, mine, mine."*

Walking further into the room I took in the huge handmade bed. Picking up one of the pillows, I brought it to my nose. Immediately my nipples got hard, and my clit started throbbing.

"Are you okay, Reggie?" I heard Jett say, from far away. All I could hear was my heart beating.

I knew my wolf was showing when I turned to him, "Whose room is it this?" I growled, panting slightly.

"Oh shit. Is Dex your mate? From the way you are acting, I'm guessing he is."

"Dex? Is this his room?"

"Yeah, it is. What can I do to help? He won't be back until late tonight and your wolf is showing. You're growling, Reggie."

I took stock and realised that I was close to shifting. I needed to find out the rules, and who we had to hide from before I could do that. I took a deep breath and moaned. *"Bad idea, Reggie,"*

I muttered to myself. *"Don't breathe him in. I need to get out of here."*

I looked at Jett "I need to get out of here. Hopefully, the further away I get, the better. Oh shit, Jett. What happens if he doesn't want a wolf for a mate? I mean you guys are all leopards. I would be weakening the bloodline."

Looking pissed Jett grabbed me and pulled me out the door, shutting it with a bang. Taking my hand, he pulled me down the passage towards the dining room.

"What shit are you spouting now, Reg? Why wouldn't he want you? You're amazing, loyal, great looking, with a fantastic personality. You're the best friend I've ever had. If my brother doesn't want you, he's bloody stupid." By now, Jett was stomping down the hallway.

"Okay, big guy. You can calm down now. It's not so bad. I had a little freak out, that's all. You do know I love you, right?" He looked at me side-eyed "Eww! Not like that you dope," I said, gagging.

He grinned "Are you feeling better now? I love you, too. You're the best friend I have, other than my brothers. I can't wait for you to set Dex back on his ass when he gets home."

"You are just a little bit evil," I said to him.

We were getting closer to the dining room and my stomach was growling. My wolf had settled down some, now that we weren't near the bedroom. I could still smell him, but he was mixed with the scent of his brothers, so it was much easier to handle.

We got to the dining room, and I saw Falcon and Zane lift their heads, sniffing the air. I could feel my face blooming red with embarrassment. Clearly, they could smell my arousal.

They both turned, looking at Jett and me with raised eyebrows. He groaned and rolled his eyes. "Would you stop? It's not me that has her worked up."

"It's not? Who is it, then?" asked Falcon.

"Dex," answered Jett.

"Dex?" said Zane, looking at me, confused, "When did they get home?"

"They aren't home yet," said Falcon. "They won't be back until tonight. Duke just phoned to check on us because Dex's leopard is going nuts." He grinned. "It's all making sense now."

Zane was still looking a little confused. While they'd been talking, I'd been loading up my plate with the delicious looking lunch and was stuffing my face.

Taking pity on him, I simply stated, "Dex is my mate."

Zane looked at me, then at his brothers. They all had huge smiles on their faces.

A big grin spread across Zane's face. "Oh, I cannot wait for Dex and Duke to get home. The Grumpy One isn't going to know what's hit him." Zane started laughing.

"The Grumpy One?" I asked.

Jett looked at me. "He isn't really so grumpy. He just has a lot of responsibility, and he had to grow up fast when our parents died. We were all still very young and he had to take over the running of this place and become a parent. Dex is a great male and I think you're the perfect mate for him."

My eyes started tearing up, and I blinked my eyes. The brothers surrounded me in a huge hug. It felt wonderful. My wolf was rolling around in glee, making me laugh. I knew she had missed having a pack. I hadn't seen my sisters for nearly six months.

"Okay, enough of this mushy shit," I said, pushing them away and wiping my eyes. "What are we doing today to take my mind off my body going crazy?"

"Well," said Jett, "I thought we'd take you to the clinic so you could see the setup, and then if there's time, we can take a ride around the property.

We'll also take you to the hot springs. You can shift anywhere here. It's a safe place, and all the staff are aware. There are baskets with clothes around the place in case you need them. We have staff that check them and keep them stocked for us. Maggie's in charge of the housekeeping. You can usually find her in the kitchen area, so if you need anything replacing, give her a shout. I'll introduce you when she is up, from her siesta. Don't worry we'll keep you busy this afternoon, Reggie."

I was relieved as my body felt like it had a live wire in it, and I knew I needed to keep busy.

And keep me busy they did. After lunch we piled on the quad bikes and drove to the clinic. It was very well stocked with everything any vet would need. Falcon explained that I would mostly be home-based, dealing with small animals that came to the clinic. Jett told me that some people drove nearly two hours to get their dogs seen to.

Falcon said that sometimes, if it was a big job, we would both go out together by plane to whichever ranch or farm needed us, and do everything from vaccinations to taking blood, as well as checking on all the customer's livestock, and their dogs and cats.

I could not wait to get started on Monday.

Getting back on the quad bikes, we drove around the property, and I quickly fell in love with the wide-open spaces. The hot springs were beautiful, and over the years benches had been added. Making it like a small oasis under the trees. I was looking forward to trying it out.

Finally, when the sun was going down, we made our way back to the main house, for showers and supper.

Falcon walked me to my room so that I wasn't tempted to go to Dex's room.

"One of us will come and get you for dinner. Wait for us. They shouldn't be too late home."

I nodded "Thank you, Falcon. I'm so glad I landed here with you all. But I'm so nervous about meeting Dex. What happens if I'm not what he wants in a mate?"

"Trust me, Reggie. Dex is going to be over the moon to take you as a mate. He may be grumpy and stressed, but he is a really good male."

Wrapping my arms around him, I gave him a big hug. "Thank you. I'll wait here until one of you comes to get me."

Falcon nodded and smiled, then walked away to the rooms down the hall.

Chapter 5

DEX

Duke and I finally made it home hours later than expected. It seemed that everything that could go wrong did go wrong on the way home.

First, we had a flat thirty minutes into our journey. I was relieved when that was fixed, and we were on our way again.

Unfortunately, we then found neighbours that had a smallholding about an hour from us. They were broken down by the side of the road, so we stopped to help. By the time we were underway again, my leopard was clawing at me and I was exhausted from fighting him all day. I could see Duke was getting more and more worried, but there was nothing I could do.

Thankfully, my brothers had kept in touch, as if they knew I needed them to, so I knew they were okay.

During the ride, Duke's phone rang, and we stopped so he could answer it. During the call, he walked away from the truck, so I didn't hear what he was saying. When he got back to the truck, he was smiling. I waited for him to explain, but he said, "Nothing to worry about, Dex. Just one of Falcon's jokes."

Eventually, we saw the lights of the main house through the trees. I've never been so relieved to see our drive.

When the vehicle came to a stop, I turned to Duke.

"Brother, I think I'm going to change and go for a run. My leopard is killing me at the moment."

Duke looked at me with that same small smile on his face.

"Before you change, come into the house. The boys want to see you. They've been worried all day, and you can meet the new vet at the same time. Two birds, one stone."

I nodded. "Okay, let's go."

Getting out of the truck I could feel my leopard pushing his way to the top as my eyesight got clearer and my senses seemed to be on fire. Inhaling deeply, I felt my teeth punching through, and my fingers tingling as my claws started extending. What the hell was happening? What was that smell? Instead of pulling me out to the open, my leopard was pulling me to the house. I took off at a run towards the dining room, where I could hear the others talking, Duke was close on my heels.

"Dex, you need to slow down before you go in there."

But I was beyond listening, everything faded except for the female that I had in my sights. She was dancing, in the arms of my youngest brother Zane. She was beautiful, with a firm, muscular body and long curly, blonde hair that fell down to her gorgeous ass.

"Hands off. Mine!" I growled.

She turned towards me, still laughing. Her eyes sparkling with happiness.

Zane quickly lifted his hands and moved back to where Jett and Falcon were standing. I saw Duke moving towards them, but he got too close to the vision in front of me, and my leopard didn't like that.

I roared as he moved towards her. He put his hands up in peace. "It's okay, brother. I'm not going to touch. Just moving out the way."

In a moment, I felt soft hands cup my face, then I looked down to see my mate's beautiful eyes staring back at me.

"Shh, it's okay. I have you."

I took a deep breath and closed my eyes. Opening them, I looked down and smiled at her.

"So beautiful."

I bent to capture her lips in a kiss, then everything seemed to disappear, as peace flowed through me. Hearing her moan as I ground my rock-hard cock against her, I could feel the precum surging. Picking her up I ground her against me, then turning, I made my way to my room. There was no way my brothers were going to see what was mine.

As we approached my room, a grinning Falcon was ahead of me, opening the doors. I was so far gone that I hadn't even seen him leave the dining room. I was grateful though, as he'd made it easier to get to the bed quickly.

Sliding my mate's body down mine, I saw her blurry eyes open, taking me in.

"I need your name," I growled at her.

"Reggie, my name is Reggie."

I laughed softly at my sneaky brothers, but I couldn't be mad when they had brought my mate to me. It was not something that I ever thought would happen.

"Welcome home, Reggie."

Her eyes filled with tears as she looked at me. "Thank you, I never thought I would have a home again."

I couldn't handle her tears, so bending down, I kissed her again and got lost in her lips. Pulling her dress over her head, I took a deep breath and drank in her unique scent. I buried my face in the crook of her neck, my teeth nipping at the tendons there.

The first time was going to be fast and hard. My leopard was tired of waiting.

I looked at her "The first time is going to be hard and fast. My leopard needs it, but after that, I promise that I will savour you."

"Hard and fast is good as long as it's soon, please," she begged.

Pulling her panties off I brought them to my nose and inhaled deeply. My teeth started punching through again as my mouth watered at her scent. Stripping quickly, I pulled her to the edge of the bed.

Opening her legs, I saw her pink pussy glistening with desire. I gave her a long lick, and her hips came off the bed as she wailed. Gripping her hips firmly, I continued to lick and suck. I added two fingers to her channel that was tight as fuck. I couldn't wait for my cock to be in her but first I needed her to cum. She started to flutter around my fingers, then she clamped down and I felt her thighs shaking. It was time.

Pulling my fingers out of her I picked her up and flipped her over. Without giving her time to realise what I'd done, I thrust deep into her and stopped. I felt her push back on me.

"Dex, you need to move or I'm going to make you move," I heard her say.

Groaning, I started to thrust, feeling my leopard come to the top. Putting my arm around her, under her breasts, I pulled her up toward me, her back against my chest. Moving her hair to the side, I licked where her shoulder met her neck then bit down breaking the skin. As I tasted her blood, her pussy clamped down hard on my cock, when her blood hit my throat. The flavour enticing. I came so hard I saw black spots before my eyes.

Slowly coming to, I realised I was still holding her tightly in place. Releasing her neck, I licked where I had bitten. I looked at my mark, feeling satisfaction in the knowledge that every male who saw it would realise she was mine.

Softly kissing her face, I disengaged.

She turned to look at me. Softly, with smile said, "My turn now."

Chapter 6

REGGIE

Grabbing him, I flipped him over my shoulder onto the bed. I laughed at the look on his face, his eyes wide. His leopard was peeking warily through his eyes, while my wolf was rolling in glee that we had managed to take our mate by surprise.

Not giving him a chance to speak, I crawled over him to take his still hard cock in my mouth. He started to moan, and then I felt a rough tongue lick my belly. Soon he was making his way with small kisses towards my pussy. I wouldn't be able to play much longer, as my wolf was pushing at me hard.

Lifting myself off him, I turned around.

"I liked that position," he said.

I grinned down at him. "69 is my favourite number, but we can play later. For now, my wolf needs her mate."

His hands gripped my hips as I centred myself and sank down on him slowly. I moaned at the feeling of fullness as I bottomed out on him. I opened my eyes and looked down. His eyes were closed, and his face looked relaxed, although I knew he wasn't from the way his hands were gripping my hips so firmly. I knew I'd have bruises in the morning.

As I sat there feeling his cock pulse within me, a burst of pure love spread from within my chest until it warmed my entire body.

His eyes shot open, and I basked in his warm green gaze. His face softened, and with a gentle sigh he turned his head to the side and pulled me down to him. He wrapped his arms around me tight as he slowly thrust up into me.

I could feel my orgasm rushing to the surface and my wolf's teeth punching through my gums. She soon worked her way to the front, then struck between his shoulder and neck. My entire body felt as if it was alive with electricity. I came so hard that I blacked out.

Coming to, I was still lying on top of Dex, wrapped tightly in his arms. He was pressing kisses to the side of my face and rubbing a lazy pattern up and down my back. Never had I felt so safe and happy. My wolf had completely retreated. I could feel her content at the back of my mind.

Dex cupped my cheek, turning my face to him, he softly pressed a kiss to my lips. Tears pricked my eyes. It had been so long since I felt so much love.

I felt him softening, and our combined juices slowly leaked out of me. He gently manoeuvred me off him and onto the bed.

With a soft kiss on my forehead, he said, "Don't move from here," and walked into the bathroom.

My eyes went to the flexing muscles in his back and thighs. I sighed happily *'My male has an awesome ass,'* I thought to myself.

He came back with a cloth, his eyes never leaving mine. Gently he moved my legs and wiped me clean with a cloth. I felt tears well again.

He threw the cloth towards the bathroom, then cupped my face in his hands.

For a time, those beautiful green eyes roamed over my face, showing concern at the sight of the tears in my eyes.

"What's wrong?"

I smiled. "Absolutely nothing, everything is just perfect. These are happy tears," I assured him.

"Happy tears or not, you need to stop. You're breaking my heart."

"Oh my god, I love you so much," I couldn't help telling him. "How is it possible to feel like this so soon?"

He got into bed and pulled the covers over us, pulling me close into his arms.

"My dad told me that it's our animals. When we meet our mate, we just know, and there's an overwhelming feeling of peace. He was completely right."

"That sums it up exactly," I said.

Snuggling deeper into his side I gave a sigh of contentment. My wolf was happy, as we drifted off to sleep finally at peace.

Chapter 7

DEX

Waking to bright sunshine, I felt more rested than I had in years, with my arms full of my woman, my hand cupping her breast. I felt lighter than I had in years.

Slowly moving her leg up towards her chest, I gently pushed inside her, finding her still wet. Once inside, I stilled, just waiting, trying not to come like a teenager. When I had more control, I rocked slowly backwards and forwards, my hand moving from her thigh to her clit.

I could tell the instant she woke up, as she clamped onto my cock so hard, I nearly saw stars. Kissing her shoulder where my mark lay, nuzzling deeper into her neck. She sighed and pushed back against me.

Slowly building the heat up, her stomach tensed against my hand as she made a low keening sound, and I felt her pussy pulse as she came. I couldn't hold back anymore, so I started thrusting quicker until I felt that tingling at the bottom of my spine and I knew I was about to come. Holding tight to her hip, I tensed as I came. Wrapping my arms tighter around her, I held us together.

Kissing her head, I murmured, "Morning baby, how did you sleep?"

She pushed back against me. I heard the happiness in her voice.

"Best sleep I've had in years. I especially liked the morning wakeup call."

I laughed. "I think the morning wakeup call might be a regular occurrence from here on out."

Feeling myself softening, I got out of bed and looked down at her. She looked content, as her beautiful eyes smiled up at me.

As I scooped her up, she squealed with laughter. "A bit of warning next time!" she laughed, looking at me.

"Where are we going?"

"I thought we could grab a shower before breakfast," I looked out the window at the bright sunshine and heard the day-to-day noises of the house and ranch. "Or lunch. We may have overslept," I shrugged.

Moving towards the bathroom I watched her reaction. My leopard loved the water, and when the bathrooms had been redone, I'd added a shower with multiple shower heads. With that and the stones, numerous plants it felt like we were in a tropical forest.

"Wow, this is gorgeous. I could live in your bathroom," she said.

Putting her down near the shower, I started the water and waited for it to warm up. I held my hand out to her and smiled. pulling her into the shower with me. I couldn't help hugging her to me as my leopard pushed forward.

Looking down at her, I watched a smile appear on her face. "Well, hello, you gorgeous feline. Are you coming to say hello this morning?" The next thing I knew, my leopard was pushing his head into her stomach rubbing his scent all over her.

Chapter 8

REGGIE

I saw his leopard in his eyes and the surprise on his face as it pushed forward. The next thing I knew, there was a magnificent leopard with me in the shower, pushing and rubbing his head all over me.

He was absolutely beautiful, and I could feel my wolf pushing to meet her mate, but it was my turn first. Lowering myself, I held on to his large head and looked into his eyes. He was bigger than a normal wild leopard, and I could saw the keen intelligence in his eyes.

"Oh, wow. How beautiful are you?" I wrapped my arms around him in a hug, he rubbed his head on me in affection.

"You want to meet her, don't you?" I asked. He chuffed and nudged me with his head. I let my wolf out to meet him, and my human self, took a back seat, as our animals became acquainted.

The two of them played in the shower for a while. My wolf had never felt so content or happy in all our years together.

Finally, they retreated and let us come forward again. I found myself being held tight in strong arms.

His chest contracted, as he let out a long sigh of contentment.

"Let's get washed and go out and see what my brothers are up to."

Nodding, I reached for the shower gel. Putting some onto my hands, I started washing his back, rubbing my hands over the expanse of his shoulders and down towards his legs. I could feel myself getting wetter and wetter, my breasts aching. He lifted his head, sniffing the air. I flushed because I knew he could smell me.

Turning, he lifted me. I wrapped my legs around his lean hips as he pushed inside of me. I moaned at the fullness of his cock. He bent his head and sucked on my aching breasts. My head fell back, as my body surged with the beginnings of another orgasm.

"Now Dex, come with me."

I felt his hot release pump deep inside me and latched my mouth onto his in a hot kiss. "Wow, is it always going to be like this?" I wondered out loud.

His body shook with rumbled laughter. "God, I hope so," he grinned at me, Slapping my ass. I yelped as he put me down.

"Come on, my wolf. I'm starving, and I need food if I'm going to keep up with you."

I grinned at him as my stomach rumbled, "That makes two of us."

He turned and got out of the shower. Once more I admired the play of the muscles on his back and thighs. My wolf gave a contented sigh and lay sated within me at the sight of our mate's bare ass as he walked away to get towels.

Grabbing one, he wrapped it around his waist. Coming back, he switched off the water and wrapped me in a towel, drying me off carefully.

Rubbing a dry towel over my hair, he bent to kiss the mark on my neck, and I shivered as his tongue rasped over it.

"Nope." I said, pulling away, my stomach rumbling again. "You promised me breakfast." I ran back into the room and pulled on a T-shirt of his.

"I need to stop by my room and get some clothes."

He nodded "Let me get dressed quickly and I'll walk you down."

I watched as he put on his khaki shorts, t-shirt and boots. He ran a hand through his still wet hair and smoothed down his beard.

"Done. Let's go."

Laughing softly, I shook my head. He smirked at me and shrugged, "You said you were hungry."

Chapter 9

DEX

I couldn't believe how lucky I was to have found my mate. Not only was she gorgeous, and already held a place in my heart but, I knew she'd connected with my brothers just as quickly.

Holding her hand, I felt a deep sense of contentment, as we walked down to her room so she could change. I realised that this was the first time since our parents had died that I didn't have an empty feeling inside. Reggie filled up the space that had been empty for so long. I knew that eventually, I'd to go back to handling the ranch everything, but for today I was going to spend time with my mate and my brothers.

Walking towards the dining room we heard the voices of my brothers as they chatted to each other.

"So, do you reckon we're going to see them at all today?" Zane was asking.

"Not sure, but if anyone deserves a break and some time to bond with their mate, it's Dex." replied Falcon.

"We can handle anything that crops up for the next couple of days," I hear Duke say. "Is there anything I need to be aware of or is there anything anyone needs?"

"I'm good," said Falcon. "I can keep things going until Reggie is up and running."

"No need for you to wait," my mate said, as we walked into the dining room.

All my brothers turned our way at the sound of her voice.

Zane looked at us with a grin on his face. "Welcome back to the land of the living. You finally came up for air."

Jett cuffed him in the back of the head. "Would you shut up."

"What? I'm happy to see them. I was worried they would dehydrate if they didn't come up soon. Am I not allowed concern?" replied Zane, innocently.

"You're such a shit-stirrer, aren't you?" laughed Reggie.

Moving her to the top of the table, I pulled a chair out for her on my right. I smiled happily at my brothers.

"Zane, not even you are going to piss me off today. I would like to officially ask you to welcome Reggie into our clan, as my mate. I know you've already felt the claiming bond. I hope you'll be happy for us."

My brothers started hooting and whistling. They all got up and one by one went to Reggie. Jett picked her up and hugged her tight. My leopard rumbled in my chest, not liking another male touching her, brother or not.

"We only welcomed you yesterday," said Jett, "but I for one am thrilled. Not only do I have one of my best friends here with me, but I get to call her 'sister'."

Next came Zane. "Welcome Reggie, I'm going to love having you with us to keep the grumpy one in line." he grinned. I grabbed him from her and put him in a head hold.

"Grumpy One huh? Who's grumpy now?", I asked, giving him laughing and giving him a nuggie.

"Okay, Okay, I give. You're still the man," he laughed. I let him up and hugged him. "It's so good to see you happy," he said quietly in my ear.

"It feels good," I replied.

"Now that those two are finished messing around." I heard Falcon say.

"Reggie, I officially welcome you to the madness that is our family. I can't wait to start working with you."

"Me either, I'm looking forward to getting stuck in," she said.

Duke moved Falcon out of the way with a shoulder bump.

"My turn," he rumbled.

I wondered how Reggie would take Duke. He was the biggest of all of us at six foot six, with broad shoulders. A lot of people found him intimidating as he was the quietest as well as the biggest.

I moved up closer to Reggie and watched them looking at each other. I could see my other brothers glancing at each other, wondering what Duke was seeing.

Just as the staring had gone on for what seemed like forever, they both blinked and smiled.

"That's just freaky," I heard Zane mumble.

Duke and Reggie hugged, and I expected my leopard to go nuts, but now that we were bonded, he seemed to have settled down.

"Welcome to the family Reggie. I'm Duke. I'm sorry we weren't here to welcome you yesterday, but I hope you'll be very happy here with us."

"Thank you, Duke," she whispered, slightly choked.

I pulled her into my arms "You okay, baby?"

"I'm fine, I'm just really happy." She smiled wiping tears off her cheeks.

"Jeesh, I'd hate to know what you're like when you're unhappy," Zane said, lightening the mood.

"Right enough emotional shit. Falcon, pass the steak," said Reggie, sitting down and picking up her knife and fork.

I watched happily, as they all settled down, passing food around, and catching up on what was happening on the ranch and with the neighbours.

In the middle of the loud conversation, I put my hand on Reggie's thigh, and sighed contentedly as her hand squeezed mine.

Chapter 10

REGGIE

The next couple of weeks were idyllic. Not only did I get a mate who was attentive and loving, I also got three awesome brothers. When Falcon and I had long days on neighbouring farms and ranches treating a variety of animals, Dex always made time to give me a call to check all was good with us.

Our nights were spent loving each other and talking. He admitted he'd missed having someone to talk to after his parents died, even if it was just to tell him that he wasn't messing up with the way he was bringing up his brothers. He had Duke and they leaned on each other, but he didn't want to burden him too much, as Duke was so much younger, but they were the only ones that hadn't left the ranch. The other three had all been away at university.

I told him about losing my parents and how hard it was being put in foster care with a human family. It's hard pretending to be something you're not, and my wolf was unsettled for so long, until my mum's friend turned up and took me in. I told him about my foster siblings and how much I missed my sisters. I'd tried to keep in contact as much as possible, but the only one that I really kept in touch with was April, as she was still in the same town, we'd grown up in. April worked in a café and was guardian to our younger sisters.

I knew he was worried about the amount of poaching that was happening, and that he and Duke had been meeting with the other three families to see what could be done. The poachers seemed to be slipping past all the patrols that had been set up.

Mealtimes were like family meetings. We all met in the dining room for breakfast, lunch and supper. I'd finally met their housekeeper Maggie, a matronly woman with snow-white hair and kind brown eyes, who ran the kitchen like clockwork. She'd been with the family for over twenty years and was a stickler for serving meals on time.

That evening we had roast beef, roast potatoes and copious amounts of vegetables, with a baked pudding for dessert. I'd never been more grateful for my shifter metabolism.

I was half-listening to the discussion going on around me. The brothers were talking about the poaching and another ranch that needed a full inoculation on their two thousand head of cattle. Falcon and I would be spending the night at this ranch, and Dex wasn't happy about it.

"Just come with us," Falcon said. "Duke, Jett and Zane can look after things here. It's only for one night."

I looked at Dex "I'd love that, even though Falcon will be there, I'd feel more comfortable with you being there as well."

Dex's eyes softened as he looked at me.

He turned to Duke, who was quietly eating. "Will that be okay, Duke?"

Duke looked up, surprised. "Of course, it's okay," he replied, frowning. "Why wouldn't it be?"

"Just wanted to make sure you're good with me leaving you to handle things, with all that's going on," Dex replied.

"Dex, it'll be fine. You need to have some fun, brother, and stop worrying about everything. We can cope. I think you forget we're all adults now."

"Talking about being adults." Zane butted in.

"Lottie called today and asked if the four families want to get together this weekend at the lake. We can barbeque, have a few beers and maybe ski. The Landrys and the Russos are going, so it's just us that needs to reply. I thought it'd be a good way to introduce Reggie to the other families."

"That sounds great. I'm looking forward to meeting all of them," I said, smiling.

"They're great people. You will like them," Duke commented.

"High praise indeed," I said smiling. "I can't wait to meet them. What's at the lake?"

Between them all they told me about the lake on the outskirts of the Russos property. Seemed it was a large dam that their father had built for them, that had always been known as *'The Lake.'* They used to get together there as teenagers, to do what teenagers do when adults aren't around. There were a couple of chalets if anyone wanted to spend a weekend there.

"Why don't we arrange for the foremen to work this weekend and take the camping stuff and spend the night?" said Falcon. "Jett and I are on call, but we'll let everyone know that if they need us, they can contact us there."

"Sounds like a plan," replied Zane, nodding. "I'll let Renee and Lottie know. They're organizing the food so we can take the bikes if you want, rather than the Land Rovers?"

Dex looked at me. "Are you okay with spending the weekend at the lake?"

I nodded, leaning over to kiss him. "I'm genuinely looking forward to meeting all your friends."

Chapter 11

DEX

It was a busy week getting everything sorted so that we could all have the weekend off at the lake with the other families.

Falcon and Jett opted to take the Land Rover filled with mattresses, sleeping bags, mosquito nets, food and drink. Even though the Moore family had said they'd provide all the food, Maggie insisted we take some of her baked goods with us. Plus, we had medical supplies and veterinary supplies we thought might be needed.

"You do know we're only going for the night?" I said to them as I watched them load it all up.

"You'll be only too happy we have all this if there are broken bones, or if there happen to be any humans there this weekend," said Falcon, looking at me.

"You know that one of the Russos will more than likely have a woman with them. Remember what happened to the last one?"

"True," I replied nodding.

The last time we'd been at the lake, the woman with Luca had managed to stand on a fishing hook, getting it stuck in her foot. Then she fell overboard, hitting her head on the way down. Luckily, we had managed to radio for a plane to come and take her to the clinic in the next town for observation. As Jett was with us, he was unable to leave, as he was the only other one with human medical knowledge. Falcon hadn't been able to make it that weekend due to a horse that went into labour.

"Okay, I think we have everything," said Zane, as he finished tying down the tarpaulin.

I felt Reggie approach from the veranda and turned to watch her come down the steps. She was dressed in tight jeans, a long sleeve button up of mine over a teal-coloured tank top, and black riding boots. Her beautiful blonde hair was still wet from the shower we'd taken together earlier. She was such a beautiful vision, one I was proud to call my mate.

My lust rose as I took in the way her breasts were pushing at her top, and how her hips swayed with every step she took towards me. As soon as she was within arms' distance, I grabbed hold of and picked her up. Her legs wrapped around my hips as I kissed her. It was as if I was starving for her, never mind that we'd only been out of the shower an hour.

"Nope, uh uh, nope," Zane muttered, trying to pry us apart. I knew it had to be him, as none of the others would have been brave enough. They knew my leopard let him get away with stuff because he was the baby of the family, and my leopard still thought of him as our cub because of how young he was when our parents died.

I still turned and roared in his face though. The look of shock on his face as he jumped away and fell over, was great to see.

Reggie started laughing with me as we looked down at him on the dusty driveway.

"Did you have to do that?" he complained. "My ass is now bruised," he pouted, duck lips and all.

I grinned at him. "That'll teach you to get between me and my mate."

He sighed, getting up and dusting off his backside. "I think I preferred you grumpy," he groused, limping off to his bike.

All the others were hanging on to each other, laughing their heads off.

I took in my four brothers and the laughter on their faces. They all looked so much happier now than they had a few weeks ago, and I knew a lot of it was down to Reggie.

I hoped that they would all find their mating experience as satisfying as mine has been.

"Enough of your shenanigans," said Duke, still laughing at Zane. "Let's get this show on the road."

Duke, Zane and I were going to ride our bikes to the lake, while Jett and Falcon were following in the Land Rover. We'd all bought off-road bikes last year so we could get around the ranch easier, sometimes it was easier to traverse the dirt roads on them rather than in a vehicle. When the rains, hit the roads became too muddy for vehicles. I couldn't wait to have Reggie pressed up against me as we rode to the lake.

I let Reggie down, holding her tight in a hug. Then I lifted my hands to her cheeks and searched her beautiful eyes, seeing them laughing back at me, her face flushed with happiness at my idiot brothers. My leopard was rumbling happily in the background at idiotic cubs keeping him from his mate.

I bent and kissed her forehead. "You ready? If you need to take a break and ride in the vehicle with Jett and Falcon, just tap my leg and we'll stop."

She nodded "I'm good to go, Dex. Looking forward to riding with you, and don't worry, if I need a break, I'll let you know."

I got onto my bike and then helped Reggie on the back of mine. She put her arms around me, and I pulled her close as the bikes started up. Duke and Zane were already on theirs, but Zane was still grumbling and muttering about his bruised ass. Checking on Jett and Falcon, I got a thumbs up that they were ready to go.

We pulled out in front of them, Duke and Zane on either side of me, both wearing huge grins. We'd travel side by side most of the way as it was dirt roads, otherwise whoever was behind us would be eating dust. Jett and Falcon would give us five minutes lead time, letting the dust settle before they left.

Relaxing into the ride I felt Reggie tighten her arms around my waist.

Chapter 12

REGGIE

We were finally on our way.

I thought they'd never stop loading stuff and messing around, although it makes my wolf happy to see them laughing and joking with each other. They all seemed to have lightened up in the last few weeks.

I was loving my time working with Falcon on the veterinary side of things. There was so much variety you never got bored, and while I was mostly doing small animal stuff, I had helped on the reserve when a pregnant zebra had been found in a snare. Unfortunately, she had died but we managed to save the foal. The foal was now being cared for at the ranch house. She also had free rein of the gardens. Falcon said we would be introducing her slowly back into the herd a soon as she was able to fend for herself.

I would be sad to see her go but obviously, in the long run, it was better for her, to be with a herd.

Hugging my arms around Dex, I felt my wolf peek out as she took everything in from the back of the bike. We both loved the feel of the wind in our faces, taking in the new scents and scenery around us. So very different from where we came from, but also very beautiful. It had been very dry, and I knew that Dex and Duke had been concerned about fires breaking out. The ranch was so far away from everything that if there was a fire, they'd need to put it out themselves. There were no fire departments out here or hotshots to help with wildfires. They had to rely on each other and their neighbours. They'd been doing all they could, setting up fire breaks and doing controlled burns. Hopefully, it would rain again soon.

I was looking forward to meeting the other families. Dex and the others had been catching me up on their history, and what they did to support each other.

I'd never encountered Hyena, Wild Dog or Elephant Shifters before. Although from what I could understood the Moore women couldn't shift into their animal and wondered at the reason.

About an hour and a half into the journey, just as I was starting to get a numb backside, I smelt water in the air. Looking to my right, I saw Duke smile, and holding up his hand to show me five minutes. I nodded that I understood.

Zane whooped and revved his motorbike next to us, then took off, leaving us in his dust. We could hear him laughing all the way. Dex shook his head and looked across to Duke who was smiling but also shaking his head.

Soon we drove under huge trees that provided some relief from the relentless heat and pulling into a cleared parking area. I took in the beautiful expanse of water that they called the lake. Lovely big trees surrounded it and there were groups of chalets with thatched roofs scattered around. There was also what looked like a kitchen, living area combination under one roof.

Dex tapped my thigh, so grabbing his shoulder I got off. As my feet the hit dirt my legs felt like jelly from sitting for so long. Shaking them out, I took my place beside my male. Bending at the waist, I shook my hair out, running my fingers through the windblown mess to untangle it. Once I was sure I didn't look like I'd been electrocuted, I tossed it back and straightened up. I felt Dex's hooded eyes on me, so I winked and blew him a kiss, laughing at his growl.

"Hot damn!" I thought as, I saw two gorgeous men coming towards us. Both stood six foot with curly black hair, wide chests, and solid muscles. With them was another male but this one was slim and wiry, with brown hair that was run through with light coloured streaks.

I saw them approach Zane and Duke and give them the usual manly hugs and back slaps that seemed to be the universal form of greeting between alpha men.

Dex come up next to me and took my hand. "Are you ready to meet the other families?"

"I can't wait to meet them, although the way you all speak of each other I think they're more family than friends".

"You're right," he said.

As the men came up to us, I could see them looking at me with keen eyes and slightly raised brows, as they saw our linked hands.

"Reggie, this is Anton Russo, Luca Russo and Joel Landry. Guys, I'd like you to meet my mate, Reggie Channing."

The men broke into big grins, and I held out my hand but none of them made a move toward me. Instead, they looked at Dex, who gave them a slight nod. His hand tightened on mine as the males came forward.

Joel was the first one up. Taking my hand, he laid a quick kiss on the back of it.

"It's a pleasure to meet you," he smiled, then moved on to Dex who got a pounding on his back and hug. "Happy for you, brother," he grinned at Dex. Moving off for the Russo brothers to come in.

I was picked up by first Luca, and then Anton who swirled me around, making me laugh.

"Right enough of that," Dex said firmly, taking me from Anton.

Anton let go of me quickly and looked worried.

"Sorry, brother," he said. "Just that you've made us so happy and given us the hope that we might all one day meet our mates."

Dex grabbed Anton's arm in a firm hold, hand to elbow, and Anton returned it.

Looking at his friend's face, Dex said, "No apologies necessary, Anton. My leopard's still on alert as the mating's still new. And, as Reggie rightly pointed out to me, we're more than friends. We're family."

There was a bunch of throat clearing from the males around me, as I took in their faces. Dex's brothers smiling were at me, and I felt myself tearing up.

"Hey, you guys are here. Finally!" A tall female about six foot with long black hair, denim cut-off shorts and a black bikini top came bounding and bouncing over. I was seriously worried about how her bikini was holding her boobs in, with the way she was jumping around, hollering at the women following her. There were three other women of a similar height as the first, and I assumed these sisters were the Moores. There was also another smaller woman, who looked a lot like Joel. They were all laughing at the dark-haired woman who was getting closer to us.

"You're finally here what took you so long."

The energy was bouncing off her and I couldn't help but smile. That was until she threw herself at my mate.

My wolf come forward, then I heard lots of shouting and felt hands on me, but my wolf was pissed off that another female had her put hands on her mate.

Then I felt Dex's arms around me as he enfolded me from behind his soft voice crooning in my ear.

"Reggie, you need to let Lottie go. She didn't mean anything by it. She was just hugging me. She's like a little sister to me. Please let go of her neck. She understands now not to touch, and I think she's learnt her lesson. Come now, come back, Reggie. There we go."

His leopard purred against my back as he kept up his continuous crooning in my ear. I came back to myself and looked down into the eyes of the female whose throat I had just had in my teeth.

She was looking at me with tear-filled green eyes. "I'm sorry. I promise I don't want your mate. It would be like wanting my brother." Genuine disgust filled her face at the thought. "I didn't know he was mated, I'm sorry. Please don't kill me."

My wolf snorted in disgust and shook her head. I heard her say it was like hurting a puppy and I laughed at her in my head as she gave me back my body. I came back, still sitting on the woman, with Dex still holding me. A hand waved a t-shirt in front of me.

"For the love of God, woman. Cover up!," I heard Zane say. "Before our brother loses it. One unexplained shift at a time, yeah?"

Grabbing the shirt, I pulled it on, realising I was completely naked and still sitting on top of the woman. I grinned down at her.

"No hard feelings?"

Lottie shook her head at me, looking relieved. "No hard feelings. I'm truly sorry. Um, do you think you could get off me? Because you're completely naked, and unfortunately, I don't swing that way."

I heard a snort come from somewhere, and suddenly everyone started laughing. Dex pulled me up from Lottie, and I put my hand out to her and helped her up, even though she towered over me.

She kept hold of my hand. "Reggie, it's nice to finally meet you." She laughed and shook my hand, then pulled me into a hug. "I'm Lottie Moore, and I'm never pissing you off again."

"Well, that was certainly interesting." One of the other Amazonian women pushed Lottie away with her hip. This one had gorgeous red hair.

"I'm Renee Moore this one's older and wiser sister and these two are her younger, wiser sisters, Ava and Maire Moore." She motioned to the two blonde twins by her side. They both came forward and gave me a laughing hug.

"Don't worry about Lottie. We've all wanted to throttle her at some stage," one of the twins said.

"Hey!" Lottie protested.

The smaller woman who looked similar to Joel came forward. "Hi, my name is Amy Landry." She held out her hand and we shook. She smiled. "I thought you may be sick of the hugs by now, so I wanted to give you a choice."

"Thank you," I smiled at her, then pulled her into a hug. "In my family, we hug though."

I felt an answering squeeze from her.

"Right, now that's all settled, let's go get something to drink and eat, and see if we have to do any damage control," I heard Falcon say.

Luca came back from the campsite. "Nobody saw anything. They couldn't see through the circle we had around the girls while Reggie was changed."

I instantly felt guilty.

"I'm so sorry. I usually have much better control over her."

Dex turn me towards him. He cupped my face in his hands, as I looked up at him, he pressed a kiss to my forehead and pulled me to him. I instantly relaxed.

Chapter 13

Dex

Turning Reggie towards me, I took her face with my hands. I saw the guilt in her face at having changed in front of so many people.

I kissed her forehead. "You have nothing to feel guilty for. We all understand what having a mate means. It's partly my fault. If I had let the others know about you before we arrived, Lottie would never have hugged me. It'll be fine, I promise."

The others quickly agreed with me.

"Come on, let's go set up and get some food." I heard Renee say. The other's started moving off, except Lottie who was looking very sorry for herself.

Clearly, she was feeling bad. We had always been close, and she was like the little annoying little sister that I had never had. When we were younger, she was always following me around, and when things were bad at home, she would stay over with us. For some reason, her father was extremely hard on her.

I kept one arm firmly around Reggie and held the other one out to Lottie.

"Lotts, come here." She shook her head. Her head was down, and her shoulders were heaving.

I felt Reggie looking at me. "Go to her," she said quietly.

Shaking my head, I pulled her with me towards Lottie.

Pulling Lottie into us, Reggie put her arm around her and pulled her in tight.

Lottie completely lost it then.

"I'm so sorry," she sobbed. "I didn't know. I would never have hurt either of you like that."

For a while, we held her and let her sob it out. I felt someone watching us, and looked up to see Renee watching us, her face looking sad. I knew then that this was more than just what had happened with Reggie. I had a feeling that this had to do with their father. Nodding at Renee, I turned to my friend who seemed to be inconsolable. Reggie gave me a worried look.

"Lottie, you need to look at me, hun. You're starting to worry Reggie. You and I both know that your being this upset has nothing to do with what happened earlier and has everything to do with your arsehole of a father. What did he say to you this time?"

She drew in a big breath and sighed. "It doesn't really matter. Just more of the usual. I'm so sorry, Reggie. This isn't how you should be meeting me. I'm not usually such a big baby."

"Hey, I don't see any babies here. I see my mate's friend who's hurting, and we can't help unless we know why." Reggie said. I fell even more in love with her at that moment. There wouldn't be many mates out there as patient or as willing to allow their mate to hold an unmated female, or be as kind to one as Reggie was being now.

Lottie heaved a huge sigh and moved her face from my shoulder. She rubbed her hands over her face and looked at my mate.

"You're perfect for him," she said. "I'm so happy for you both. You've given every single one of them hope that there is someone out there for them."

"What about you?" asked Reggie.

"Who me?" Lottie laughed. "I doubt that anyone would want to take on this mess. No, I'll leave that to my sisters."

"Lotts." She must have heard something in my voice because she looked up at me.

She smiled softly. "Don't worry about me Dex. You know me. I'll bounce back. I always do, don't I?"

"You shouldn't have to, Lottie. I don't know what your father's problem is, but he needs to stop."

"You know how he is. Hopefully, he won't be here that long. I think he has another woman. I just hope to God he doesn't bring home another baby. I think Renee might have a fit." I knew she was trying to make light of it all.

Reggie was frowning. I knew she was picking things up and I would explain my side to her when we were alone. For now, there was nothing I could do for Lottie unless she came to me.

"Okay, but just know that if you need to come to us, you can come. We have room, and I can work something out with Renee, so he doesn't have to know," I said.

Reggie was nodded her head. "What he said."

"I know, and thank you. I'm still sorry though, for what I did."

"It's done. We forget about it from now," said Reggie.

"Okay, let's go get a drink and some food, because I'm starving." We moved off, me keeping Reggie in the curve of my arm. Lottie moved to her other side, where I saw my mate take hold of Lottie's hand and squeeze it.

Pressing a kiss to Reggie's temple, I whispered to her, "I love you."

Smiling up at me, she pressed a kiss to my jaw. "Love you too."

Chapter 14

Reggie

We walked towards the others who were sat around a fire pit that was ready to be lit later that evening.

Renee motioned to us. "Food and drinks are over there in the rondavel. Help yourselves."

We walked over to the large round structure. It had a huge evergreen tree coming out of the middle of its beautiful, thatched roof, and a gorgeous stone floor. A wall about thigh-high went all around it, with spaces for the doorways. It was cool under the shade of the roof. At one end there were comfortable couches, armchairs, and sectional tables.

A large dining room table and chairs were in the middle, while at the other end there was a hand-carved wooden bar. The wall behind the dining table was covered with beautiful African prints and wooden carvings. There was also a sideboard laid with food covered by a net to keep the flies off.

There was plenty of cold meat and salad and what looked like freshly baked bread.

"Wow," I said turning around trying to take everything in. "This is gorgeous. Who would have thought this was hidden away here?"

Dex chuckled "It is something, isn't it? We don't use it enough. Come grab some food. The girls always make sure there's plenty. Do you want to eat in here, or out with the others?"

I looked out at the others all sitting around either on camping chairs or on the low wall that surrounded the fire pit. They were all chatting and laughing.

Lottie seemed to have settled down now and was sat on the wall between Duke and Jett. My wolf was feeling bad for what had happened, even though it was perfectly natural. She kept showing me a sad puppy, and I had to agree that for such an Amazonian woman it was still a bit like kicking a puppy. I decided then that I would make sure to spend time with Lottie. She seemed to need the contact and reminded me of some of the touch-starved children that had come through our foster home.

"Let's eat with the others. It'll be nice to get to know them."

Dex nodded.

We loaded up our plates and walked out to the others, sitting in the dappled shade. Finding a place to sit, I noticed that Falcon and the other brothers already had empty plates.

"Did you even chew your food, or did you just inhale it?" I asked laughing at them.

"Hey, it's not our fault you guys took a scenic tour getting here." grinned Jett, nudging Lottie slightly. She gave a little chuckle and nudged him back.

I sat eating and listening to the conversation. Apparently, there was a busy afternoon of skiing, boating, or fishing if you wanted to.

It was hard to believe that this oasis existed out here in the middle of nowhere, so I took my phone out and took some pictures to send to my sisters. I knew that April would get a kick out of it, and I planned to send them to her, as soon as we were back at the main house.

Amy sat down next to me and offered me a cold drink.

"Thank you," I said, taking it from her.

"You look like you need it. Are you okay, or have we completely overwhelmed you?"

"Oh, I'm okay, thanks. Just taking it all in. It really is beautiful here. I'm going to send my sister some photos when we get back."

We got to discussing our families, and at one point, I felt Dex drop a kiss on my head as he moved off with the other guys. It looked like they were putting the boats in the water. The other girls came over to chat, and I knew straight off that we would be great friends. They were all so down-to-earth and didn't seem to realise how beautiful they all were.

I found out about how each family ran its farm. Amy and Joel were the only ones on the Landry farm at the moment, as their parents had gone on a trip around the world, now that youngest child was in university. None of the other Landry siblings were interested in running the farm and had all moved away.

The Moore girls ran their place, despite their father's interference, although it seemed he wasn't home very much. From what I could understand this wasn't a bad thing as he only seemed to turn up when he needed money or to use Lottie as a punching bag.

Anton and Luca were all that was left of the Russo family. Their parents and three younger siblings had been killed while the boys were away at university. The MacGregor parents had run their place for them as well as their own, until the boys had graduated and moved back home.

"Hey!" we heard a shout from down by the shore.

The guys were waving at us from the boats.

I sighed looking at them. They had all stripped off and were just wearing shorts. Muscles were flexing and glistening as they moved around getting everything ready. My wolf gave a little whine.

The girls fell about laughing as I slapped a hand over my mouth.

"Yeah, they are a pretty hot bunch of guys. I guess we don't see it because we grew up with them and it's too much like looking at our brother's, even if they aren't our actual brothers," laughed Amy.

"Exactly," grinned Renee. "I mean, they get hit on all the time when we go into town, but I guess we're immune to their charms."

Dex came running up soaking wet, and I did start drooling then, which sent the girls into another fit of laughter.

He shook his wet hair over us, causing the others to curse at him. Then he grabbed my hands, pulled me up and threw me over his shoulder, and carried me off, with a slap on my ass.

"Hey!" I tried to protest, but I was laughing too much. The others got up and followed us, all still laughing. On the way, Renee grabbed a bag full of with towels and other stuff, that being the kind of organised person she was.

I had an absolute blast that afternoon. We went from water-skiing, to racing each other on jet skis.

Eventually, as the sun was setting, we called it a day. It was one of the best days I'd had in a long time. I couldn't help wishing that my sisters had been there to enjoy it with me.

Chapter 15

Dex

It had been a perfect day. I hadn't laughed so much in years or been so relaxed.

Reggie had fit right in with all my friends. Jumping in with racing jet skis against Anton, Luca, Joel and my brothers.

The girls all seemed to like her too, and I noticed her make a concentrated effort to include Lottie in all things.

We now had the lake to ourselves, as all the visitors had gone home. Only a few people were allowed to use the facilities, and they had to book their time through the Russos. This evening there was no one but the four families.

We were around the fire. I was on a cushion on the floor with my back against the wall, with Reggie between my legs resting against my chest. She had her head turned and was listening to something Renee was saying.

All around us were my brothers by blood, and my brothers and my sisters by choice. Everyone was laughing and happy, without exception. My leopard let out a rumble of content, which brought answering rumbles from my brothers. Which in turn made the others grin.

"I wish it could always be like this," said Ava, who was sitting on a chair next to Marie, as always.

"Yeah," echoed Amy, with a smile.

We left it at that, just taking time to enjoy the sunset with good friends and family.

Pretty soon we were called in to supper by the caretaker who, along with his family, looked after the properties when the Russos weren't there.

We could rely on the fact that the beds had been made and that all our clothes were unpacked and put away in our chalets.

Supper was roast chicken, potatoes and vegetables that had come from the gardens on the property. We sat around the dining room table under solar power lamps that were hung at intervals away from the table, so we weren't bothered by moths. One of the benefits of being a shifter is that we aren't bothered too much by mosquitos.

As we were finishing supper, we heard a vehicle approaching. Everyone stood, and Ava and Marie dimmed the lamps, so our eyes could adjust to the darkness. Renee unlocked a cupboard on the wall by the bar and took out the guns kept there. I felt Reggie move next to me, so I took hold of her hand.

"What's wrong, Dex?" I could hear the edge in her voice.

"Just being careful, as it's unusual for us all to be together like this. What with the poachers amping up their activities, we're just being cautious."

She nodded.

The vehicle stopped and parked by the other vehicles. I didn't think it was anyone to worry about, but you never can tell.

Many of us moved out into the darkness and spread out.

"Stay here with the others. The Moore's can't shift, so they have guns. If there's a threat, you can change. All the people that are left here are aware of what we are".

"Okay, Dex, be careful," she said quietly.

I felt my leopard pushing forward. My sight sharpened in the dark, and I lifted my head and to if I could smell who it was, but the wind was blowing the wrong way.

Going forward into the dark towards the car park, I felt my brothers around me. Up ahead I could see Joel, and to my left were Lucas and Anton.

As we got closer to the vehicles, I recognised the Land Cruiser parked crookedly next to ours and wondered which of the Whyte's was in it. The Whyte's were a family that owned a small fish farm that shared borders with the Moore's and the Landry's. It was only Kyle and his mother who ran the farm, his father having passed away when Kyle was about five.

Kyle's mum was in the driving seat. She had her head on her arms and I could see her shoulders shaking.

I went to the window and knocked. She jumped and looked at me with a white face, one eye swollen shut.

"Dex, thank goodness. I hoped that the foreman had been right and that you were all here. We were attacked tonight, and our staff and Kyle need medical help. They broke our radio, and I couldn't get hold of anyone."

By now she was shaking. I reached in an turned off the ignition then opened the door. Jett pushed me out the way so that he could get to her. He started asking her questions, and Amy arrived with his bag.

She looked at me. "I heard her from the dining room," she pointed at her ears. "Wild Dog remember?"

We all returned to the dining room where Renee and Lottie had coffee and whisky waiting.

Mrs Whyte was in a complete state, insisting we didn't have time for coffee, and that her family needed help.

Reggie approached her and took her hand. Kneeling next to her, she said gently, "Mrs Whyte, is it?" She got a nod.

"Mrs Whyte, I understand that you're upset, but before we can go to your place, we need to know what's going on so that more people aren't hurt. We need to know what medical supplies to bring. Can you help us with that? Okay?"

I watched as Reggie got her calmed down enough to make sense and get the information from her.

As Reggie and Mrs Whyte talked, Jett was cleaning her wounds and cuts, and the others were gathering what we needed in firearms, food and drink. We were unsure what we would find when we got there, but it sounded as if the manager's house had been burnt down along with the village around it. The main house was untouched as it was so far away from the village.

I was getting angrier and angrier as I listened to her. The attackers had been after the fish, and Kyle had told them to take as many fish as they wanted.

Somehow a fight had broken out between the foreman and the poachers.

Kyle had intervened but had got shot in the process. It was while the poachers were burning everything down that Kyle had grabbed his mum and put her in the car, telling her to find us. He'd gone back to help their staff.

He'd told her he had only suffered a flesh wound, but she thought it was worse than that.

I looked at the others, who nodded.

"Reggie, I need you to stay here with Lottie, Ava and Marie. As you're the only other one here who's trained in human medicine, you'll need to set up a triage system. Renee and Amy, handle the food, as we'll bring all that we can back with us. Jett, Falcon, gather as many medical supplies as you. Anton, Lucas you're with us. Joel, you need to get on the radio and inform the local farms and our foremen on to be ready for trouble. Also, get John here with the plane, in case we need to fly anyone to the main hospital in town. Then you should, follow us with extra water and food if we aren't back by the time you're done."

I went to Reggie and hugged her tight. Looking down into her worried eyes, I said, "Be careful. Listen to the others. They know the area and the people. I'll be back as quick as I can. This is not quite how I wanted to spend the evening."

She shrugged. "You be careful too, and keep in touch so we know what to expect, okay?"

I nodded, then pressing a kiss to her lips. We all scattered to do what we needed to do.

Chapter 16

Reggie

My heart was beating so fast in my chest. My wolf was agitated and not happy that Dex had left us. He was right though; I had a year's training in human medicine before I'd changed to veterinary. I was definitely capable of setting up a triage system.

I went with Lottie to see what they had and was surprised at the number of medical supplies on hand.

Seeing my questioning look, Lottie said, "It's because we're so far away from hospitals, we are used to sorting ourselves out."

Following my lead, she grabbed everything we needed and went back to the dining room. Ava and Marie had set up tables and had woken up the caretaker and his family. They were busy gathering together blankets and towels.

Amy had got Mrs Whyte some sweet tea, and she was looking much better. She was helping Joel, who was on the radio, contacting everyone in the area.

I was still in shock that we had gone from an idyllic family day to an emergency situation.

I was also proud of how quickly Dex had assessed the situation. Known each person's strengths and where they would best used.

Once we had everything set up, it was just a case of waiting for the injured to start arriving.

Lottie had persuaded Mrs Whyte to take some painkillers, and she was now sleeping on a couch with her head on Lottie's lap, covered with a blanket. At first glance, I thought she was in her fifties but now that her face was relaxed in sleep, I realised she was younger. She didn't look much older than forty-five. I wondered how old her son was.

Joel was still by the radio listening to the chatter. It seemed the poachers had made a getaway, or were in hiding, as the wildlife rangers couldn't find them.

Zane came over the radio. "Joel, are you there?"

"Copy that, Zane. Go ahead."

Gone was the light-hearted Zane we were used to. In his place was an angry-sounding male.

"Jett is on his way to you. Ten with minor injuries and Kyle who still has a bullet in his shoulder. There isn't enough light here for him to remove it, and he'll need help from Reggie on this one."

Joel looked over at me. I nodded, then started moving to get everything as ready as I could.

"Roger that, Zane, Reggie will be ready for Jett when you get here. Any other news?"

"Two fatalities. They were caught in their homes and didn't make it out in time. We have nearby neighbours stopping in to help. Give Renee, Lottie and the twins a heads up. Their father is one of those with minor injuries."

"Okay, Zane. They are here and are prepared."

"Dex, Falcon, Duke and I will be coming in later on foot. We're going to make a sweep to see if we can find anything."

"Roger that, Zane. We all heard. Stay safe. Out."

Out of the corner of my eye, I noticed the Moore sisters tense up at the news that their father would be coming in and Lottie seemed to close off completely. I also saw that Mrs Whyte was sitting up. She must have been woken by the radio.

I watched as different emotions seemed to roll over her face. After a while she seemed to make up her mind. She stood up, turning to Lottie. She bent down and took Lottie's face in her hands. Neither of them said anything, they just looked at each other. Lottie's sisters looked at each other in surprise, watching the scene unfold.

Something must have passed between the two women, because Lottie's whole body seemed to relax. Mrs Whyte nodded, kissed Lottie on the head, and stood up straight.

I hadn't realised how tall she was. She'd seemed so frail when she arrived, but now that she had calmed down, you could see she stood strong, ready to do battle.

She turned to look at us and took a deep breath. It was clear that she was cataloguing different scents. I hadn't realised that she was a shifter, and looking at the surprise on the other's faces, neither had they. Almost all her injuries were now completely healed after her sleep.

"I know you're all surprised that I'm a shifter. It's a long story for another time. And I know you girls are surprised that I know so much, but I was friends with each of one of your mothers. I know you don't know me or Kyle, and that's our fault. We tend to keep to ourselves, and because we're quiet nobody notices us much when we go out. Once everyone is sorted, I'll tell you more. Okay?"

I nodded. "Mrs Whyte, I do need to know if Kyle is a shifter, because if he is then the bullet wound may have healed over already."

"Please call me Annie. Kyle is a half shifter. His father was human. He doesn't heal as quickly as a full shifter, which is why I was so worried."

I nodded. "Okay. Thanks for telling me."

Amy came in from the car park. She had been on watch.

"They're about a kilometre out, so should be here within the next ten minutes."

I knew the next couple of hours were going to be busy, so I went outside. Looking up at the stars in the clear bright sky, I could smell the smoke in the distance, and I said a little prayer that all those out looking for the poachers were kept safe.

Chapter 17

Dex

I hated to leave Reggie, but she was best off staying behind where her medical skills would be needed.

We all jumped into one of the vehicles and took off towards the Whyte property.

In the distance, we could see the fire glowing, and smell the smoke in the air.

Lucas was flying down the road as fast as he could, given the condition of it. I made a mental note to discuss fixing them at the next family.

Thanks to Lucas' skilfully reckless driving, we made it to the Whyte farm in forty minutes rather than the hour it would normally have taken. What we found was organised chaos.

Kyle was in the middle of it shouting out instructions, his shirt covered in blood. I always forgot how big he was, he stood around six foot three, and with the same blond hair as his mother. Most of the families didn't give much thought to the Whyte's, as they were so quiet, and kept to themselves unless someone needed them. They both had helped several families in need, but then melted smoothly into the background.

As we all jumped out of the vehicle, he turned toward us. I could see the relief on his face.

"Thanks for coming. Mum made it to you okay?" he questioned.

I nodded. "She's fine and being looked after. Suffering a bit of shock, and very worried about you. Where do you need us?"

"The injured are over there by the garage, as it's the cleanest and has a roof over it. We've got a bucket brigade going trying to put out the fires, but I don't think we'll be saving much. The main house is far enough away that it hasn't been touched. I have the staff up there getting food for the rest of the volunteers. Some of the neighbours are rounding up the horses and the other animals we had to let out in case the fire spread."

He looked me in the eye and said, "I know what you and your brothers are, so you and the Russos might better off helping the wildlife rangers in tracking the poachers."

I wondered how he knew what we were. He saw the question in my eyes.

"Something for another day, Dex."

I nodded at him.

Jett walked over to have a look at Kyle's arm. You could see it was useless, hanging by his side, and side all covered in blood.

He shook Jett off. "I'm fine. Please check on my staff. You can sort me out after all this is done."

Jett went to protest but took one look at Kyle's face and knew he wasn't going to get anywhere.

Sighing, he shook his head and moved off towards the garage and the wounded people there.

"Kyle, tell us where's the safest place to change. Anton, can you and Luca go with the rangers?"

The two Russo brothers nodded. "Yeah, no worries. Be safe." They ran over to the rangers who were getting ready to move out in vehicles to pursuit those not on foot. We would go after the ones on foot.

Kyle gestured to me. "This way."

My brothers and I followed him into the darkness. Our night vision meant it didn't make any difference to us, but clearly there was more to Kyle than we thought, because the darkness wasn't bothering him either.

He finally came to a stop by a huge tree. Pulling on a rope that was anchored to the base, a basket came down.

"Put your clothes in there and pull the basket back up. Nobody will touch it."

"Thanks, Kyle." I grabbed him by the shoulder and felt him tense up. "You do know we have to discuss this when it's all over."

He sighed. "Yeah, I know, but once you understand why nobody knows, I don't think it'll be a problem. Good luck out there and be careful. I need to go and make sure all my staff are okay, and then get to my mum."

I nodded. I could feel the impatience coming off my brothers. Quickly stripping, we all changed and made our way into the night.

It was strange us all being together like this. It didn't happen very often as our animal sides were solitary creatures. Then, as had happened when we were young and learning to hunt in this form, we fell into sync with Duke taking the lead as the best hunter. We spread out until we caught the scent of the poachers that had left on foot.

It wasn't long before we found the trail. We broke into a run moving quickly through the trees, hunting. My leopard was angry. He wasn't happy having his mate so far away when there was danger around. He wanted to get this done and back as soon as possible. I was in full agreement with him.

About an hour in, we came across a running stream. Sniffing at the water it smelled clean and fresh. We all stopped to drink before carrying on.

We finally lost the trail where it crossed over into the river. Changing back all our chests were heaving, we took a minute catch our breath.

Duke was standing near the riverbank looking at the other side.

"What do you think?" I asked him, quietly.

He pointed to the other side where a canoe was moored.

"So that's how they got across. Do we chance it?"

He shook his head. "No, too many crocodiles in these waters."

Falcon and Zane moved up next to us.

"Let's go further up. If I remember correctly, the river narrows a bit, and we may be able to cross," said Falcon.

The others nodded. We changed again and moved on following the course of the river, listening to the night's sounds around us. Up ahead we could hear the water running over the rocks where the river narrowed. Finally getting there we took stock. The water was running fast, but it wasn't impossible, our leopards were strong swimmers. I motioned with my head for Duke to go ahead, then once he was halfway, I nudged Falcon to go. He chuffed at me and made his way slowly across. By now Duke was waiting on the other side.

I nudged Zane who growled at me, so I nipped at him to teach him a lesson, reminding him I was still the oldest. He finally growled one last time and started to make his way over. I followed when he was halfway across, not wanting him to feel like I was hurrying him. My leopard didn't care that he was an adult. To us he was still our cub.

When I made it across the river, his leopard was still glaring at mine. Falcon nudged him with his head, and we continued on. I knew when we changed, I'd be hearing about not babying him.

Duke suddenly took off and I knew he was on to the scent. We heard them before we came upon them. They were laughing and joking. It looked like the alcohol had been flowing for a while, even though we were only an hour behind them. The camp stank with decaying meat and there were piles of tanned hides mixed with horns on one side. On the other were raw skins being worked on by three women. The camp was lit only by firelight, and all the men were armed with rifles.

We hunkered down watching, hoping they would pass out soon from the alcohol they were consuming. It was locally brewed beer by the looks of it, so I knew it shouldn't take too long. I wondered where the vehicle had gone.

Just then a radio went off, relaying the voices of what we assumed were the others in their group. They were speaking in the vernacular but having grown up here we could understand them.

It sounded like they had gotten away but had to go to the nearest town as they had a few with injuries. This was good news for us, because it meant we only had the ones in the camp to deal with.

My brothers and I changed back to human and stood up slowly. I knew it would throw the poachers when the four of us came out of the bush completely naked. I hoped it would give us the upper hand.

I motioned to the others to surround the camp as much as possible.

When we were all in place, I let out a bird call that we all knew.

Three answering bird calls came back to me. I noticed one of the women had been alerted by this. I also knew that the women in these camps weren't treated very well and hoped that this was the case here. Showing myself briefly, I made eye contact with her and put my finger on my lips. She nodded in understanding. She whispered something to the woman on her right, who nodded in turn, then whispered to third the woman.

They slowly moved back from where they were working and disappeared silently into the trees.

Creeping slowly up to the men we managed to subdue and disarm the majority of them quickly. However, one took us by surprise when he came out of the hut running towards Falcon with a Machete. There was a shot from the trees, and he dropped clutching his leg. One of the women came out trees holding a rifle in her hands looking proud of herself. The rest of the women brought us some ropes to tie them up with. All the time the men were shouting at them. We finally gagged them.

Looking at the three women all I saw was the relief on their faces.

I spoke to the youngest one. She had been the one to take the shot at the poacher and who seemed to be their spokeswoman.

She told me that they had been taken from their village four days ago, and all they wanted was to go home. One of the women came to us with spare wraps that they used to wear around their clothes to protect them. Thanking them, we wrapped them around our hips.

We all chuckled softly when we overheard one say to the other that we must be mad, running around naked in the bush. That the fire on our heads, meaning our hair, had fried our brains.

Using the poachers' radio, we managed to contact the Russos and the rangers. They said they'd get to us as soon as possible.

While we waited, we disabled the camp. Gathered all the traps one place. We burnt as much as we could.

I had never been so happy to see the lights of the rangers vehicle. It had been a long night and I couldn't wait to get back.

We arranged for the rangers to get the women back to their families, and let them know that if they needed help with anything they should let us know. The chief ranger assured us that they had a second vehicle coming, and they'd load up everything and take it back to headquarters with them.

Processing the prisoners and the evidence meant it was going to be a long night for them.

I didn't want to stay and wait for them to process everything as I wanted to get back to Reggie as quickly as possible. We still had to collect our vehicle from the Whyte's farm.

 Looking at my brothers, and Anton and Luca, I asked, "Do you want to stay and get a ride back? I'm going back on foot as it will be quicker, than waiting for them to process everything."

We all decided that we'd go back on foot. Going back into the trees, we waited for the Russos to strip and change. Making a bag with the wraps the women had given us, we took their clothes and tied them to their backs, so they had something to put on when we got back to the Whyte's farm.

Chapter 18

Reggie

Amy, Joel and I went to where the vehicles had stopped.

We started helping everyone back to the rondavel and the better lighting it provided. The injuries seemed to be mostly minor burns, and some cuts that needed to be stitched.

I knew there was a second vehicle coming in, but it hadn't arrived yet.

Joel and Annie Whyte were talking to some of the workers that had arrived on the first vehicle. Those we had already seen were now at the table being given tea and sandwiches.

"How's Kyle?" I heard Annie ask one of her staff.

"He's coming on the next vehicle. He's hurt but he didn't want the doctor to look at him. He said the doctor must look at us first."

Annie nodded her head, and then started making her rounds of all of them, assuring them that they could trust me, even though they didn't know me.

During all this Lottie was amazing, calming the scared children and making them laugh, while I bandaged and checked them over.

Other than minor injuries they all seemed relatively happy and healthy. Obviously, they were scared. After all, their whole world had exploded overnight, but I knew that we'd help to get them back on their feet.

We'd just finished with the first load when we heard the second vehicle coming in.

I felt the tension rise among the Moore sisters. This was the vehicle their father was on.

I wondered what he was like. If he was an Elephant Shifter, I knew he would be a big man. All the girls were six foot.

I heard him before I saw him, my hackles rising at the tone of the voice on one of the men. I saw Annie say something to one of her members of staff, and they all started filtering away into the darkness. Soon it was only the few of us left.

Annie made her way to stand next to Lottie and her sisters; they all stood shoulder to shoulder with their faces blank and waiting.

Out of darkness, I saw a huge blond male approach us. His face was hard, and his eyes looked furious. He was at least six foot three, broad of shoulder with muscular arms and legs. His long blond hair was tied up in a man bun. His left side was covered in blood and his left arm hung stiffly by his side.

I assumed the man behind him being helped by two large men was the

Moores sister's father. By looks of him he had broken his leg. His face showed little other than hard living and bitterness. He was cursing and swearing at the two males who were trying to help him over to us.

Both of these males were tall, well over six foot five, with dark tanned skin, bright green eyes and bald heads. They were clearly brothers. The only difference was that one brother had a scar from a cleft lip.

My wolf had woken up and was taking this all in slowly rumbling in my chest. It was clear she didn't like the look of the Moore male.

I was grateful to see Jett coming in from the vehicle, even though he was looking just as irritated as the males that were accompanying the male with the broken leg.

The two males took him to a chair and dumped him not gently onto it.

The blond giant approached, and Annie quickly moved towards him. Then I realised that this was Kyle Whyte. Finally, he had made it to his mother. I watched with a smile as Lottie's eyes seemed to eat him up as he approached them. She didn't seem to realise she was still gripping his mother's hand and had been tugged forward when Annie moved.

I watched the interaction between mother and son, and could feel the love flowing between them as he bent and put his forehead against his mothers'. He looked into her eyes the same way that Annie had done with Lottie. They did this for a minute, and then smiled.

"Mama." It should have seemed strange, hearing such a big man call his mother *'Mama'* but the moment was so special.

Annie patted his face with her hand and spoke.

"I'm glad all my boys are safe," she smiled.

Kyle moved back from her and let the two bald males who had come in with him move forward. They each went through the same ritual with Annie.

I could see everyone wondering who they were, especially when they all called her *'Mama'*.

I knew they couldn't all be hers as Annie was only in her early forties and these males were late twenties.

From another part of the room, Mr. Moore was shouting and swearing. I knew some of this was because he was in pain, but I think it was mostly just his nature to be difficult.

Jett had set his leg and was administering pain relief which I knew wouldn't help much as he would burn it off too fast.

"If you don't calm down, Frank, I'm going to give you a sedative," Jett said, firmly. "We need to sort Kyle out as he still has a bullet in his shoulder."

Frank Moore continued his angry shouting. "This is all their fault anyway. If they had better security this wouldn't have happened."

Jett looked at me over his patient's head and rolled his eyes. There were a few hidden snickers.

"Reggie, can you give Frank some more painkillers please," Jett asked, "and then can you help me look at Kyle's shoulder?"

"No problem." I replied making my way over to them.

I went to pick up the painkiller, which was when the stupid old bull decided to open his mouth.

"I'm not having some idiot nurse touch me. She probably doesn't even know what she's doing. Who is she, anyway? Are one of you copper knobs fucking her?"

I heard shocked gasps behind me.

The Moore sisters shouted "Dad!!" almost in unison.

Jett and Joel looked fit to kill.

That look decided me. Enough blood had been shed tonight. Instead of the painkiller I picked up the syringe, filled it with from the sedative vial, strode over and jabbed it into his arm. Despite his outrage, he was snoring in minutes.

"Oh, thank fuck, Reggie," said Jett. "I didn't think he'd calm down enough to let me do it."

I shrugged and grinned at him "That's why you're a doctor and I'm a vet."

There was a round of relieved laughter.

We made our way over to Kyle. Lottie had already had him take his shirt off and had cleaned up the wound. Because he had shifter genes from his mother he had already healed over, and I knew it would hurt as we'd have to open the wound up again.

Jett looked at Kyle and Annie, "We're going to open this up again to get the bullet out. It's going to hurt like a mother fucker, and I don't have any more lidocaine left to numb the area. You're going to have to hold very still as I don't know what damage has been done to your shoulder blade."

Kyle nodded grimly.

I sighed, looking at him "Kyle, you have to tell us that you understand, and we're going to have to hold you down to do this. Are you ok with that?"

Kyle looked me straight in the eye, "I understand. My brothers will hold me down," he said nodding toward the two huge males that had come in with him.

"Okay, let's get started. If you two could hold his legs and his other shoulder down. Lottie, you're the best nurse we have. Go to his head and hold it still until we need you. Annie, it's best that you're not here to see this. It's going to be painful, and we don't need you going nuts. I know he's an adult but that doesn't seem to matter to shifter," I smiled sympathetically at her.

She nodded. "It's enough that Rory and Sean are with him, and Lottie will keep him calm."

"So that's what your names are," I said looking at the two men standing on the other side of their brother.

Jett made his way back to us with his hands gloved up.

"Your turn," he said to me.

Finally, we all got into position with the Rory and Sean holding his legs and shoulders and Lottie at his head.

Lottie had made her way to the top of the table and was looking down into Kyle's face, his cheeks between her hands. They seemed to be staring at each other much the same way that Annie and Lottie had earlier. I was wondering what type of shifters the Whyte's were. I saw his two brothers look at each other with raised eyebrows and then smile, they all seemed to relax.

Jett looked with a confused look on his face. I shrugged.

"Right," said Jett "I'm starting now."

As he started to make an incision, Kyle didn't even flinch. After the initial cut, it was quick work. The only time we heard anyone speak was when Kyle said, "Don't cry, baby girl. It's okay."

That's when I realised Lottie had tears running down her face as we worked on Kyle.

Ten minutes later the bullet was out, and Kyle had already started healing. "You should be fine within twenty-four hours," Jett told him. We all breathed a sigh of relief.

Unfortunately, that was about the moment Frank Moore decided to wake up.

I heard a groan go around the group as he started shouting and swearing.

"Lottie, Lottie where are you, you stupid useless female. Bring me a whisky."

Renee went over to him, waving Lottie away.

"Dad, you can't talk to Lottie like that. What is wrong with you?"

"Don't you tell me how I can talk to my daughter, Renee. It's because of her that I'm stuck with females and no males to take over. That useless female that she is, she's only good for serving and she needs to bring me a whiskey. Lottie!" he shouted.

I watched as Lottie went towards her father with a glass of whisky.

"It's okay, Renee. Here, Dad, drink your whiskey and we'll get you home."

I watched as he went to take the whiskey, but instead knocked it right out of her hand. The glass hit the floor with a crash whisky and glass going everywhere. Then he backhanded Lottie across the face. He may have been old but there was a lot of power behind that hand. Lottie flew across the room hit the half wall and slumped down on to the floor. My wolf went crazy within me and I didn't even try to stop the change.

Even so I wasn't quick enough. I felt something fly past me toward the old bull elephant. My wolf retreated, knowing would be taken care of.

I made my way to my friend who was lying on the floor with Jett crouching to check on her. Her sisters and friends surrounded them.

"Reggie, I need you to change, and come and help me," Jett barked.

Chapter 19

Kyle

We were finally on our way towards the lake.

In our vehicle, was Jett, the doctor brother of the MacGregors, myself and my two adopted brothers Sean and Rory, unfortunately for us the old Bull Elephant Shifter from the farm that bordered our farm was with us. He'd broken his leg when he hadn't listened to us and had walked over one of wooden bridges connecting the fishponds. They had been damaged by the poachers and he had gone straight through one.

He hadn't stopped bitching and moaning since we left. I couldn't wait until we got to the lake. I was hoping my mother was okay and not too badly injured. My shoulder was hurting from the bullet lodged in it and I couldn't move it.

When we finally arrived, I went in before the others. Jett had all his medical equipment and my brothers said they'd help bring in the old bull.

I walked towards the rondavel and saw my mother standing next to four tall females. I knew that they must be the Moore sisters. It was the dark-haired one standing next to my mother, gripping her hand that got my attention. She was gorgeous. Even though I wasn't a full shifter, my animal had always been with me. He was pushing at me hard tonight and if I could have shifted, I would no longer be standing here as a man.

Making my way to my mother, I put my forehead against hers, something we've always done. I felt her love flowing between us. I didn't keep her long as I knew she'd want to see my brothers.

"Mama."

Just one word, and I knew she'd know all was okay.

My mother patted my face with her free hand and spoke, smiling.

"I'm glad all my boys are safe." I don't think my mother knew how beautiful she was when she smiled. I always felt bad that she'd never found someone else to love her like she'd loved my father, but she always said she was happy with her lot.

I let her go so she could greet Sean and Rory. I went over and sat down next to a free table that had surgical equipment on a tray next to it.

Jett was setting the old bull elephant's leg and he was carrying on shouting and making a nuisance of himself. I saw a smallish blonde woman go over to them.

I'd noticed her mating mark when she brushed past me and realised, she was

Dex's mate. I smirked, looking at my brothers as we watched her handle the obnoxious bull and knock him out with a sedative.

From the corner of my eye, I watched as the dark-haired beauty, that I'd noticed before come timidly towards me. Considering her height, this was something to watch, I wondered how often she had to make her way around unseen.

When she got to me, I saw she was gloved up.

"I need to cut off your shirt and clean up your wound so that Jett and Reggie can get the bullet out."

Her voice seemed to spark something in my animal. He was bounding around in my head, making me wince with the amount of noise he was making.

"Sorry," she said in a low voice. "Does your head hurt?"

I heard a snicker from Sean who had come to stand behind me. "Yeah, brother, does your head hurt?"

He was laughing so much that he didn't see my mother come up behind him and flick his ear.

"Boys, do I need to separate you?"

"No, mama, we were just checking on our little brother," he grinned at her.

I heard my angel snigger next to me. Looking at her, I saw her eyes were laughing at us.

Jett and Reggie approached me. They both bent to examine the wound that my angel had cleaned up for them.

I already knew they would have to open me up again to get the bullet out, as being half shifter I had already healed.

They were discussing removing the bullet without any pain relief as they had run short, and how much it was going to hurt. I wasn't paying them much attention as I was too focused on the beauty next to me.

I nodded at them, as if I had heard every word. It was only when Dex's mate Reggie sighed impatiently at me that I realised they needed me to pay attention.

"Kyle, you have to tell us that you understand, and we are going to have to hold you down to do this. Are you okay with that?"

I looked her straight in the eye. "I understand, my brothers will hold me down," I said nodding towards Sean and Rory.

They both nodded in confirmation.

I was relieved when I heard Reggie ask my mum to leave. The last thing we needed was my mother shifting. She nodded back at Reggie and Jett.

"It's enough that Rory and Sean are with him, and Lottie will keep him calm."

'Huh, that was interesting. My mother had just given her approval on my angel.' I thought.

After my mother left, I lay down so and they all went to their designated positions. My angel, I know knew her name was Lottie was at to the top of the table and was looking down into my face holding my cheeks between her hands. Her beautiful green eyes were shimmering as she gazed down at me.

"Right," said Jett. "I'm starting now."

Jett started to make an incision, but I was so enamoured by the gorgeous female above me that I hardly felt him making it.

My angel, on the other hand seemed to feel everything, and I watched as her eyes filled with tears and dripped onto my face. She was breaking my heart. "Don't cry, baby girl. It's okay," I reassured her.

Finally, they were finished, and I felt myself healing as they stitched me up. I knew that within twenty-four hours I would be healed up.

I heard a groan go around the group as Frank Moore woke up shouting and swearing.

'That sedative didn't last long enough.' I thought.

He started shouting for my angel to bring him a whisky. I was ready to punch him with the way he was shouting and demanding.

I felt my angel tense up and her hands start to tremble, she moved away from me.

By now I was on my feet. I had a bad feeling in the pit of my gut. And I knew my brothers must have as well because they came to stand next to me. I watched as the doctor and Joel moving towards the bull elephant to try and calm him down.

One of Lottie's sisters was talking to him.

"Dad, you can't talk to Lottie like that. What is wrong with you?"

"Don't you tell me how I can talk to my daughter, Renee. It's because of her that I'm stuck with females and no males to take over. The useless female that she is, she is only good for serving and she needs to bring me a whiskey."
"Lottie!"

I wondered how it could be Lottie's fault. My angel went towards her father with a glass of whisky and offered it to her father.

Then, he went to take the whiskey from her, but ended up knocking it right out of her hand. The glass hit the floor with a crash spilling whisky everywhere. Frank backhanded my angel across the face. He may have been old, but there was a lot of power behind that hand. I watched as my angel flew across the room, hit the half-wall and slump down to the floor.

I saw Dex's mate change into a wolf, but I was faster. I could feel my gorilla going mad. I didn't have the ability to fully shift but my face and hands part-shifted when my emotions were heightened, and I was angry. And I was angry, very angry.

All I wanted to do was kill. I grabbed him by his neck and threw him across the room with a roar. I stalked to where he had fallen, I could see the whites of his eyes as he watched my aggressive approach. I picked him up by his throat and held him up against the wall.

"You will never touch her again," I growled.

I turned his face towards where the others were working on my angel. There was a large pool of blood flowing from under her head. While I knew part shifters could survive most injuries, I also knew we could still be hurt so badly that we didn't always make it back to normal.

I looked into the males frightened eyes. "I can't kill you because you're her father, but I am telling you now that you had better pack your bags and leave. Because if she dies, then there will be no saving you. Trust me, my brothers and I know all sorts of ways to make you hurt."

I shook him furiously.

"Do you understand?" I asked him. He nodded his head, his face turning purple. I noticed his other daughters did not seem concerned about him at all. They were holding onto each other while Jett and Reggie worked on their sister.

He started to say something, but I stopped him from speaking.

"LEAVE!" I roared at him. I knew my gorilla was showing in my face. I released him and he fell to the ground. Picking himself up, he turned and hurriedly limped off.

My shoulders slumped as I turned to find out what was happening with my angel.

"What the fuck is going on?" I heard someone shout from the car park.

Turning, I saw Dex, Falcon, Duke, Zane, and the Russo brothers coming towards us.

I ignored them and fell to my knees next to my angel. Her eyes were shut, and she was so pale. All I could see was the pool of blood under her head.

Jett and Reggie were working quickly to get an IV set up and had already secured her neck. I heard them call for a plane so she could be taken to the hospital in town. I knew the clinic on the MacGregor farm wouldn't be able to cope with the type of injuries she had.

I felt my brothers' hands on my shoulders, holding me still. I hadn't realised that I was rocking over her or that my gorilla was constantly rumbling at them. I wouldn't have touched Jett or

Reggie as I knew they were helping her, but Sean and Rory knew our animals could be unpredictable.

By now everyone was around her, waiting and watching. My mother had come back into the rondavel when all the fighting was going on and I could see her animal in her eyes watching my angel. She put her arms around the younger sisters.

Amy was holding onto the older Moore girl who looked like she could faint at any time.

By now Dex had Reggie in his arms, and I was surprised at the grief on his face as he looked at my angel. By the tears streaming down her face his mate seemed to be just as upset as he was.

A bit later Falcon told us that the plane had landed in the field behind us and that we needed to get her there without moving her neck too much.

My brothers had already thought of this and had brought a door from somewhere.

Jett nodded. "That'll work. Kyle, are you coming with us? I'm assuming you are, as it seems like Lottie is your mate?"

I nodded at him. There was no way I wasn't going to be on that plane.

"Okay, you need to change your shirt because going into a hospital all covered in blood is going to raise questions."

He hadn't even finished talking before Rory had given me his shirt.

"Go. We'll make sure everything is sorted here."

I pulled them both into a hard hug and kissed my mother on her cheek. I stopped by Lottie's sisters before getting on the plane.

"I'll make sure she's okay. I have warned your father that he has to leave the area by tomorrow morning. Let my brothers or my mother know if he hasn't left."

They nodded and replied, "Thank you."

Chapter 20

Dex

We finally made it back to the lake to lots of shouting and screaming. My leopard was frantic when he heard our mate's howl, and I knew she'd changed.

I could see the others hurrying. The Russos would have to catch up as they weren't as fast as us when shifted, but I had to get to my mate.

Shifting back to human, I grabbed a pair of shorts from the basket and took off towards the dining room. I heard my brothers behind me and in the distance, the yipping of the Russos in their Hyena form.

Running up to the dining room I saw that Kyle had Frank Moore up against the wall. Frank's face was turning purple, but what surprised me the most was Kyle's face. He wasn't fully shifted but his face had changed, his nose had flattened and broadened, his incisors had grown and his entire body had bulked out with muscles.

He roared at Frank "LEAVE!" Frank turned and hurriedly limped off.

"What the fuck is going on" I shouted.

Then I saw Lottie lying on the floor with a pool of blood under her head. Jett and Reggie were working at speed to get an IV set up and had already secured her neck in a brace.

Kyle went to Lottie and hunkered down at the top of her head, not touching her as Jett and Reggie worked on her.

I heard Joel say that the plane was on its way. Two big males put their hands on Kyle's shoulders holding him still. His animal was constantly rumbling.

I didn't think he would hurt them, but I moved closer to Reggie just in case.

Everyone gathered around while Jett and Reggie stabilised Lottie. I was still wondering what had happened.

Looking around, I saw Annie had an arm around each of the younger Moore sisters.

Amy was holding onto Renee, who looked like she was going to pass out any minute.

Reggie stood and came up to me, her eyes filled with tears. I put my arms around her and held her tight.

"What the hell happened?" I asked.

She wiped at her eyes. I felt my brothers, Anton and Luca come up behind me.

"Frank went nuts, demanding that Lottie bring him a whisky and telling her it was her fault he didn't have any sons to take over from him. Then he knocked the glass out of her hand spilling the whisky that she had been bringing him. And then backhanded her with all his strength. She flew straight into the wall and hit her head, hard. Her skulls definitely fractured and she's lost a lot of blood. She hasn't woken up since. Kyle went after Frank," she paused a moment, "I think he's Lottie's mate."

Falcon came and told us that the plane had landed on the closest runway, which was in within walking distance. We needed to get Lottie there somehow, without moving her neck too much.

The two men with Kyle had already thought of this and had brought a door from somewhere.

"Who are they?" I asked Reggie.

She shrugged "Annie says they're her sons."

That surprised me because the males looked a couple of years older than Kyle.

Eventually, Lottie was safely on the plane. Kyle stopped by each of his brothers and his mother. He talked to Renee as well and she nodded at him in agreement.

Jett came over to me and Reggie, gave us both a hug and kissed Reggie on the forehead.

"Thank you for your help tonight. I couldn't have done this without you. I'll call as soon as I know what's happening with Lottie. You all need to get some rest. I'm sure her sisters will want to come to town tomorrow to see her."

"Go, Jett. Don't worry, we'll sort things out here. Keep us informed."

We watched the doors on the plane close, then stood in the darkness as it took off.

I looked around at everyone who was left behind. The Moore girls were physically wilting, the twins leaning on Annie. Renee was huddled between Anton and Luca. Joel and Amy were with Kyle's brothers. Rory and Sean had

Amy tucked between them in their arms, with Joel to their right.

"Right," I said. "Let's all get some sleep and make our plans in the morning. We won't be able to do much until full light now anyway. There should be extra sleeping bags and pillows in the rooms. I'm not sure if you all want to sleep in the rooms. If you want, you could grab mattresses and sleep in the dining room?"

"Dining room," Reggie said, "I need to be with everyone tonight."

Renee nodded in agreement. "If you guys will get the mattresses, we can get the sleeping bags and pillows."

A half-hour later we were all settled on mattresses. It was now going on four in the morning, and I knew we wouldn't be getting much sleep.

Reggie was cuddled tight against my side, with her head on my chest.

She lifted her head to look at me and I could see her eyes glistening in the night.

Turning, I pulled her into me and kissed her, pouring all my love into it. My leopard was purring, trying to comfort her. Her wolf peeped out now and then, looking unsettled. I knew that she would be feeling it hard. Lottie had been accepted by her wolf and was now part of her pack.

Kissing my way down her neck to her mating mark, I licked at it. She shuddered and burrowed in closer. Her eyes closed and soon her body relaxed into sleep.

Looking up, I saw my brothers watching, making sure that she was okay. I nodded at them, and we all settled down. I knew none of us would sleep properly, as there were males with us that we didn't know.

Although if they were with Annie and Kyle, I knew they must be good males. Still, it was hard to relax.

My leopard chuffed at me, as if to say, *'Rest. It will all be explained in the morning.'*

Chapter 21

Reggie

I woke to heavy rain and soft murmuring voices. Opening my eyes, I could see the heavens had opened up and the rain was hammering down. I smelt the scent of rain hitting the hot dry ground. There's no smell like it, it seeped in and soothed the soul.

I sensed Dex still asleep behind me, his arm tight around my waist. I knew that he, his brothers and Anton and Luca would be exhausted after the number of kilometres they'd covered last night.

In front of me was someone I assumed it to be Zane because he was in leopard form. I couldn't be sure because of all the mixed scents in the area where we were sleeping. Lifting my head, I saw

Jett and Duke, still sleeping, then footsteps coming slowly up behind me. Tilting my head back slightly, I saw Falcon coming up barefoot.

Quietly he asked, "Do you need some help getting out of there?"

I nodded. I had no idea how I was going to get out from the huddle of males that had surrounded me during the night.

Holding my hands up to Falcon, he took a firm grip and pulled me out. No sooner was I out than Zane had moved into my spot, his leopard purring loudly. He sounded like a tractor.

I was trying to hold my laughter in. Falcon had no such qualms and was videoing Zane on his phone.

"For blackmail later," he winked at me.

I was still trying to stop laughing as we made our way over to the dining table.

Annie was already up and someone had brought in toast, coffee, tea and fruit. I was ravenous.

"Morning, sweetie," Annie said, squeezing me, I leaned into her slightly, enjoying the closeness. It made me realise how much I missed my foster mum. Suddenly I had gone from being happy to feeling tearful.

Annie pushed me back slightly and cupped my face. Her own face broke into a huge smile.

"What?" I questioned feeling confused at the emotions running through me.

"Your scent has changed," Annie said.

"What do you mean my scent has changed?"

Falcon looked like a light bulb had gone off in his head. He came closer and took a sniff at me.

I was starting to get a little annoyed, even my wolf was feeling confused and had started pacing agitatedly in my head.

"What the hell, Falcon!" I said, louder than I'd intended, because the next thing I knew, Dex was behind me growling and pushing his brother away from me.

"Okay, let's all calm down," Annie said, trying to calm the situation.

"Why are you sniffing at my mate?" Dex by now was part shifted, his leopard pushing hard, and I knew he was only holding back because of who Falcon was.

Falcon took a couple of steps back away from me.

By now everyone was awake, and I could feel them all around me, the tension thick in the air.

Falcon just kept grinning and Annie hadn't stopped smiling.

"Somebody better tell me what the hell is going on," I yelled. "What do you mean I smell different?"

I heard Dex's leopard rumble behind me. His arms came around me so tight my wolf made a little noise of discomfort when Dex's arms banded around my breasts.

He bent his head into the crease of my neck and inhaled deeply.

His leopard gave a huge roar. By now, my wolf was going crazy wondering what the hell was up with all of them.

I pulled myself out of his arms and jumped on the dining room table, trying to get higher than them.

Slamming my hands on my hips, I looked at them all. Every single one of them had huge grins on their faces, including the two behemoths that had come with the Whytes.

"I'm not saying it again. What the hell is going on with you lot? Would someone please like to explain?"

Amy came forward. "You mean you don't know?" she queried looking confused.

I looked up to the ceiling, taking a deep breath and huffing it out.

"It's way too early in the morning for this and I haven't even had breakfast yet. Has the whole world gone loco? I need some coffee before I go nuts on someone's ass."

"Babe, who are you talking to?"

I looked down at Dex, who had moved closer to me.

"I'm talking to the roof, because it's making way more sense than the lot of you. Did you all smoke something last night?"

"You honestly don't know?" Dex asked looking perplexed.

"I tell you what I do know, Dex. Is that if someone doesn't tell me what I don't know, I may just let loose on you. You haven't seen me lose my temper yet," I glared at him.

He put his hands on my legs and looked up at me with a smile that reached his eyes.

"Babe, I hate to tell you, but you can't have any coffee."

'Seriously.' I thought to myself he was starting to piss me off. *'Telling me I couldn't have any coffee, where did he come off telling me I couldn't have coffee?'*

"It's not good for the cub or pup."

"Hold on," I put my hand up. "What do you mean cub or pup?" My wolf by now had caught up and was doing happy circles in my head. I on the other hand, the human part of me, was still confused and my wolf didn't seem to be inclined to explain it to me.

"Brother, I think you may have to spell it out to her. She's not clued in," Duke said was smiling at me in amusement.

Dex by now was grinning wildly. Zane had his phone out and was recording us. Everyone but me seemed to get the joke.

Dex pulled me off the table into his arms.

Holding my face between his hands, he said lovingly, "Reggie, you are going to be a mother."

I felt my eyes go huge. "Oh!"

He nodded.

"Oh!" I couldn't seem to get my brain to work properly. It was like it was stuck on a loop.

His shoulders started shaking with laughter as he bent his head to kiss me, long wet and deep. Now, this I could get behind.

"Thank you," he whispered in my ear.

I think it hit me then that I was pregnant. My wolf was rolling her eyes at me. Like she had room to talk.

Standing in the middle of that dining room with the rain beating down and cleansing everything, I felt my heart swell with happiness.

I felt more arms around me as Dex's brothers joined us and for no reason, I burst into tears.

Annie started laughing. "Get used to it. It's going to be a roller coaster of a couple of months. Come sit down and have something to eat. You'll feel better and you can tell us how you didn't know about your scent changing."

We made our way to the table, but there weren't enough seats, so Dex pulled me onto his lap, where I was quite happy to snuggle down. I noticed that Amy was pulled into the lap of one of the twins. I wasn't sure if it was Rory or Sean.

Joel didn't look all that pleased, that is his sister seemed to have been commandeered but was keeping quiet for now.

As we started passing plates and food around, I explained about growing up in foster care after my parents had died.

"Didn't your foster mother tell you though?" asked Amy.

"I'm not sure if she knew. They couldn't have cubs of their own which is why they fostered so many. They did adopt our two youngest sisters before they passed on. My sister April is their guardian."

"But not you?" Annie queried.

I shook my head. "My parents had made them my guardians so there was no need for adoption. My foster mother was my mother's best friend growing up. I was happy with them and had a good childhood. I had a lot of siblings. They were great parents and I miss them every day."

"Foster mothers are sometimes better than your actual mother," one of the twins said.

Annie smiled at him and cupped his cheek with her hand. "That's because my boys are easy to love."

"Talking of your boys Annie, can we please know who's who?" I can't keep calling them Twin One and Twin Two in my head," I asked.

She nodded and looked at the males next to her.

"Sean and Rory are the eldest of my sons. You can tell them apart because Sean has a scar. They aren't my natural children. They were birthed by my sister. When they were born, she refused to bond with Sean and only wanted Rory."

Taking a deep breath Annie continued, "I wouldn't stand for that, so she told me if I wanted them that badly to take them and leave. I was only sixteen going on seventeen at the time and I don't think she thought I would. I took them and what money I could get my hands on and left. Worked odd jobs for about a year."

With a faraway look on her face, she continued with her story. "I came here when I answered an advert for a housekeeper and was hired by Kyle's father. He was in his late thirties by then and his wife had recently died. I realised very quickly that he was my mate, but he wouldn't touch me until I turned eighteen. He was human and didn't understand about mates. To him, I was too young. That was a tough year for me," she laughed softly.

I saw her face soften as she thought of him. Rory reached over and held her hand.

"He was such a good man. He never treated the boys any differently than Kyle. We had Kyle a year later. He left the fishery to all the boys, not just Kyle. As far as he was concerned, they were all his sons."

She wiped her eyes on the tissue that Amy handed her.

"Why have we never met them before?" Dex questioned.

Annie sighed. "My sister. I'm not sure what you know about Gorilla Shifters, but I'll try and explain the dynamics and how they work. There is always a male in charge of the family, and he has a handful of strong females under him that are only for him to mate with. They are not mates though, this is just to ensure his bloodline continues."

Annie's face twisted with a look of disgust on telling us this, taking a deep breath she continued.

"When they were about ten, she decided she wanted them back. The reason being the male she was under had died and the boys were the only male offspring she had. Family members that I was still in touch with let me know and I managed to hide them. She only wanted Rory and that wouldn't have been good for either of them. All her other children were females and they needed males to take over the family. So, we kept them hidden on the farm and when we went and registered Kyle's birth, we registered them at the same time to show me as their mother and my mate as their father. When they were eighteen, they joined the military and have only been back home for about two months. The last ten years that they have been gone have been the longest ten years of my life. My sister passed away this year, so they can no longer be called upon to take over the family, it's fallen to the next nearest male relative. And that male is not going to come looking for competition. Sean and Rory have let them know they don't want anything to do with the family business."

We all sat back, completely blown away.

"Wow," I said. "I want to be Annie when I grow up."

Everyone started laughing, including the twins.

I snuggled deeper into Dex as they all started chatting among themselves about what was to be done today. My wolf and I were content to bask in the knowledge that we were safe, had a mate who loved us and a pup or a cub on the way.

I felt my eyes grow heavy and close, comfortable and safe with those I already considered family.

Chapter 22

Dex

I felt Reggie relax into me and looking down I realised that she'd gone back to sleep. She looked so peaceful, with a small smile showing on her face. My leopard was purring, feeling proud that our mate would sleep feeling safe, while surrounded by so many that did not make up our immediate family.

I looked up to see Annie smiling at us.

"She will do that a lot in the next couple of weeks until the pup or cub is bigger."

I sighed, suddenly missing my parents and all the wisdom they could have imparted to us in this situation.

Annie gently touched my fingers that were resting on the table.

"You don't need to worry. Your mate is strong and if she needs a females perspective, I am only an hour down the road or on the phone. You're both going to be fine."

I nodded at her. Seeing the others were finishing up with breakfast, I decided we better find out what was happening today with the clear up and getting everyone back home.

"What's the plan for today?" I asked, looking around the table.

Annie sighed.

"We need to get back home to see what's salvageable and if we have any fish left to fill next week's orders at the restaurants we supply. Repairs will need doing and staff housing will have to be sorted out."

"Okay," I nodded, hitting my glass with my fork to get everyone's attention. "Let's do this. The Moores' need to go into town to the hospital to check on Lottie, as we've not heard anything back yet. If Anton and Luca could go and check on the Moores' place and make sure the old man has left before the girls get back from the hospital. The rest of us, including Joel and Amy will go back to the Whytes' and see what is needed and what we need to help with."

Everyone nodded and agreed with the plan, then started the process of packing up.

Annie went to speak to her staff members that were still around, to make sure they were all okay and well enough to travel. We'd try and make everyone fit into the vehicles we had or come back and collect them later.

Looking down into Reggie's sleeping face, even with all that was going on, I felt a huge sense of peace.

I felt a touch on my shoulder and looked up to see Renee.

"I'm so happy for you, Dex. I wish you both only happiness."

I squeezed her hand as her eyes filled with tears.

"Lottie will be okay, Renee. She's a tough cookie. She'll be home causing mischief and chaos before you know it."

She nodded, wiping at her eyes. "I just wish I knew why our father hates her so much? The rest of us he treats indifferently but Lottie he hates."

"I think you need to speak to Annie. She seems to know what is going on."

"I will as soon as we're back home and Lottie is with us. I think she needs to be there for that for that chat."

Ava and Marie came up next to Renee, their backpacks full.

"We're ready to go." Ava said. The twins had puffy, bloodshot eyes from crying.

I nodded "I'll come and say goodbye in the car park. Let me just wake Reggie. She'll want to say goodbye."

I felt a poke in my ribs and looked down to see her glaring at me with her beautiful, mismatched eyes. "Reggie is awake thank you very much. I was just resting my eyes."

"Of course, you were," I nodded seriously.

I groaned as she got off my lap and gave me an elbow in the stomach.

I watched as she walked over to Renee, Ava and Marie, her rounded hips swinging in time with her hair which she'd left down, it was hanging long and curly just past her hips. I adjusted my cock in my pants. Hearing a snort, I looked up into Rory's eyes as he smirked at me.

I shrugged. "What can I say? She's, my mate. And I'm not sure why you are looking so smug. You have to still go through Amy's family. Do you have any idea what Wild Dog Shifters are like with their offspring? Assuming she is your mate of course and she better be after the way you two have been acting around her."

Rory just smiled at me as he looked over to where Sean was helping Amy pack and clean up.

"She is. And nothing will frighten us away," he replied.

I nodded "Good. Because her family is great, unless you hurt one of their offspring or one of their siblings."

Getting up, I walked over to the parking lot. Amy had joined the females and they were all in a huddle, arms around each other Annie included a group hug.

My brothers come up next to me on one side, Anton, Luca and Joel on the other. Rory and Sean stood next to Joel. We watched as the women all put their heads forward until they were touching, seeming to draw strength from one another. As one they took a deep breath, let it out, then slowly stepped back. All the Moores' looked much better after that, and all were slightly smiling.

Renee, Marie and Ava got into their Land Cruiser and arms appeared out of open windows as they waved and drove away.

Annie stood between Amy and Reggie with her arms around their waists.

With a quick squeeze to each girl, they turned to us, all of them smiling brightly.

Reggie updated us. "Were ready to get going if you guys have everything you need. Annie just took a call from Kyle. Lottie is doing better and will hopefully be home by the end of next week. He's staying in town with her until she comes home. Renee and the girls are going to spend the night in town and will be home tomorrow. Can you update their foreman please, Anton and Luca? Jett is going to make his way home this afternoon and should be there by the time we get back."

It was like a huge cloud had lifted and we all breathed easier on hearing the news.

Clapping my hands together, "Okay, then. Let's get to the Whytes' and see what needs doing to get them back up and running."

Chapter 23

Reggie

After getting the update on Lottie we all felt hugely relieved. Annie had reassured Kyle that they could manage the fish farm and get everything sorted. She told him to stay with Lottie.

After packing, clearing up and making sure the caretaker had everything under control, we got into our various vehicles and motorbikes and travelled to the Whytes' farm.

In the light of day, you could see the devastation that the fire had wreaked on the property. The staff quarters had been hit the hardest. Luckily, we weren't in the winter months and had, had rain so it wasn't as dry as it could have been. If they had hit the farm in the middle of winter the fire would have spread much quicker.

The fishponds seemed largely to be unaffected, so the orders would still be fulfilled the following week. I knew this was a relief to Annie.

Annie, Amy and I made our way to the main house, which luckily had not been touched by the fire. It was a gorgeous colonial-style house with a massive front veranda, covered in plants and comfortable furniture. It was beautifully cool under the veranda roof.

Walking into the house, we stepped straight into a wide foyer. To the right was a door leading into a massive lounge with a large fireplace and a big comfortable sofa and chairs.

To the left, there was a corridor to the bedrooms. Ahead of us was the kitchen which is where we headed. Like the rest of the house, it was large and spacious, with wood cupboards and bright sunflower yellow curtains. There was a large table off to the side surrounded by eight mis-matched chairs. The whole place had a lovely comfortable homely feel to it.

Annie made her way to the coffee pot and put it on, put water into a kettle and put it on the stove.

"Welcome to my home," she said smiling proudly.

"It's beautiful, Annie," Amy said, from the window, where she was looking over the abundant number of herbs on the windowsill.

"There's more outside," Annie said pushing open the back door, followed by the screen door. We traipsed outside.

Directly outside the door, there were flagstones covered with a lean-to roof and a large vegetable garden. Off to the side were fruit trees including lemon, lime, satsuma, papaya and mango.

Amy's face was slack with amazement. "Oh Annie, this is just wonderful."

Her fingers brushing gently against the plants, Annie took our hands and led us around the corner, where there were three huge greenhouses filled with seedlings.

It was like a secret oasis. We had gardens back on the ranch but nothing like this. It was amazing.

"What do you do with all your produce?" I asked with interest.

"Most of it goes into town to the restaurants and hotels that buy our fish. Then there's a basket a day to each of our staff. I do canning, I pickle some and I make jam and marmalade that I sell in a couple of the tourist shops in town."

"This is truly amazing, Annie." I was in awe looking around at her enterprise.

She gave a little shrug but looked pleased with the compliments.

"Come, let's get you some jams and sauces that I made last year, and you can tell me what you think. I've been working on some new recipes, so I need honest reviews before I take it to market."

She took us to a storage unit that she unlocked. Inside, it was beautifully cool with shelf upon shelf of bottled and labelled jars. To the left, was a labelling set up and journals with handwritten notes.

Annie noticed me looking at them and said sheepishly with a small smile, "The boys keep telling me I need to keep my notes on the computer, but there's just something so comforting about writing everything down."

Grabbing a wicker basket from beside her desk she went to a shelf and started loading an assortment of jams and sauces into it. To show she was serious about feedback, she attached a form to each bottle so we could write our notes on it.

Going back to the kitchen, she grabbed a couple of boxes and loaded them up with the jars from the wicker basket. One for us at the ranch and one for Amy and Joel. I couldn't wait to get started on trying them.

Annie looked at us seriously. "Don't forget, I need honest feedback. If you don't like anything, please tell me why, so I can adjust recipes or just scrap them all together."

Amy and I agreed that we would give each item honest feedback. A bit later we got to discussing other items that Annie wanted us to try, while she made sandwiches for lunch. Once the males were back from making basic repairs and noting what needed to be done most urgently, we would have lunch. Her next recipe was for chilli sauce, but the chillies weren't ready to be harvested yet.

I was in awe of this female, and I knew my sister April would love to meet her. She was so easy to talk to and before I knew it, both Amy and I had told her our life stories and she was laughing with us.

The back door opened up and the males came trooping in, banging their boots and wiping them on the mat by the kitchen door.

My eyes caught Dex's, and I smiled widely at him, feeling happy.

Chapter 24

Dex

After making the rounds with Sean, Rory, Joel and my brothers.

It was decided that the most important thing to do was getting accommodation set up for the staff, as almost all their homes had gone up in flames because their homes all had thatched roofs. We decided that tents would be the quickest thing for the moment.

Rory and Sean decided that if they were going to rebuild from the ground up then it would be best to completely move the staff quarters away from the fishery. This way the homes would not be so easy to target as they would be further away from what the poachers had been after. Setting fire to them had caused massive confusion and panic and that is how the poachers had got away.

The staff agreed, so we picked a spot under the trees where there had previously been offices, that had since been demolished. This meant there was water and electricity nearby.

Phoning Jett as he was still at the hospital in town with Lottie. I arranged with him to go and pick up as much camping equipment as he could from the camping store to bring it with him on the plane. He was to come to the Whytes rather than go home. He could ride home with us.

Once this was all sorted, Rory and Sean took us on a tour of the property.

The set-up they had in the workshop was amazing. Joel whistled in admiration as we came across the motorbike that was lying in parts on the floor. There was artwork all over the walls and a spray-painting booth with tools lined up neatly on benches across the back wall.

 "This is Sean's baby," Rory told us. "He made a name for himself with his art in the military and has done the design and painting for a couple of custom bikes. It's a pain to get them shipped out and costs a fortune, but luckily the people commissioning them aren't short of money."

Taking a deep breath, he said, "That's Sean's, but this is mine."

Opening the double doors to the right of the workshop he took us into a woodwork shop complete with power saw, circular saw, jigsaw and mitre. It was a similar set-up to the workshop, with the big equipment on one side and the smaller tools all on the back wall.

There were half-finished projects on one side and completed projects on the other side.

"We take orders online and try and consolidate shipments with the bikes, so they can go in a container to help keep costs down."

I looked at him. "Well, Rory, I'm going to need you to build me a crib. This stuff is seriously amazing. Does Kyle do anything? You guys are making us look boring as fuck." I joked.

Sean laughed and for such a quiet guy he had a booming laugh. Because it was so unexpected the rest of us started smiling like total fucking loons.

"No way. Kyle does the fish and is fucking awesome at numbers and making money, so Rory and I get to do what we like without worrying about all that."

Rory cleared his throat and grinned at us. "He does do some pretty amazing leatherwork in his free time though. Says it relaxes him."

This started us all off laughing again. Even the brother who wasn't artistic, was artistic! Rory took us over to Kyle's set-up which was in a small area in the corner of the room, with some pretty impressive leather work hanging up.

I shook my head in wonder as we left, the twins locked up the different doors to keep all their work safe.

In this case, it was true about still waters.

We made our way back to the house to update Reggie, Amy and Annie on what had been decided on the accommodation.

Instead of going around to the front door, Rory and Sean took us in through the back door past the largest veggie garden I have ever seen. It put ours to shame and ours was nothing to sniff at.

Stopping under the lean-to roof that covered the back door they turned to us.

"Make sure you wipe your boots on both mats before going in, or Mama will have our hides and trust me as sweet as our mother is, her tongue is sharp when she needs it to be."

We nodded looking at each other. Our mother had been the same and Maggie was the same, so maybe it was a female thing.

After wiping and cleaning our boots we walked into a massive kitchen dominated by a huge table that looked like it was definitely made by Rory. The mismatched chairs were strange, considering Rory's skills, but they suited the room.

I looked up, catching sight of Reggie. Her beautiful, mismatched eyes sparkling with happiness as she smiled widely at me.

"Are you all sorted now?" she asked.

"All sorted babe," I said stopping by her to drop a kiss on her mouth.

"Let's grab the sandwiches and drinks and make our way to the veranda. You boys can fill us in on what's been decided," said Annie.

All of us grabbed something. I noticed Amy and Reggie had small cardboard boxes and I wondered what was in them.

Making ourselves comfortable, I decided that I'd get Rory to make some furniture for the veranda at home, because ours was not nearly as comfortable.

With Reggie snuggled up next to me, eating a great lunch with a truly lovely family, even with all that had gone on last night, I felt true contentment.

Looking at my brothers sitting, or in Zane's case sprawled in a hammock, I saw the same contentment in their faces.

We chatted, learning about this new family. We told them about the four main families meeting once a month and invited them all to the next meeting.

It was late afternoon when the plane did a flyover to let us know to meet them at the airstrip about a kilometre away.

We went and offloaded the tents from the plane and took them to the staff members to help set up. Kyle had included a big mess tent that included gas stoves, tables and chairs. There was also bedding and an assortment of clothing that the Moore females had sent.

We left the staff to set up their temporary new homes. They seem a lot happier that they had the night before. It was wonderful to see.

As I watched Reggie and Amy hug Annie goodbye, I knew we would be seeing more of this family, especially with all of Annie's sons having found their mates among the females in our friend group.

Chapter 25

Reggie

I was so tired that I hadn't made a fuss when Dex suggested that he and I ride back in the vehicle with Jett and Falcon would take his bike.

Slightly, squished between the two large males I felt safe and content after an afternoon spent in wonderful company.

My eyelids began to droop and as I jerked my head up for the fourth time, I felt Dex's arm come around my shoulders pulling me down towards his lap. Lifting my legs, I put them across Jett's lap and with my mate's fingers combing through the top of my hair and massaging my scalp, I fell asleep.

I woke to the familiar smell of our bedroom and Dex gently pulling my clothes off. Seeing me awake, he leant over and gave me a long, wet, sweet kiss.

"Hi love, how are you feeling?"

I grinned up at him "Horny." I murmured.

He laughed softly at me, "Well, we can't have that."

Bending down, he licked across one of my nipples. His tongue was slightly rough, so I knew he had let his leopard out slightly. I shivered and arched up towards him. He lost no time in sucking my nipple deep into his mouth, while plucking my other one getting it nice and hard before moving across to the other one.

By now I could feel myself getting wetter and I knew Dex could smell what he was doing to me.

His fingers were at my pussy, flicking slightly at my clit before dipping inside. By now I was writhing all over the bed. I didn't think I could hold on when my orgasm hit me hard, making me see stars.

He played me until I calmed down. When I looked at him again, he was between my legs looking up at me, his Leopard showing in his eyes.

"Again," he growled.

Licking me from top to bottom, I felt his fingers enter me and pump a few times as his tongue flattened against my clit. I felt myself gathering for another orgasm when took his fingers out of my pussy. H pushed one of them gently into my rosebud. I tensed and he stopped, waiting for me to relax, letting him in. With his finger in my ass, I felt his tongue push into my pussy and his thumb press down on my clit. I felt so full, with his fingers in my ass and his tongue in my pussy, I detonated and came so hard that for a second all I could do was feel.

Coming to, I was panting so hard my wolf was whining softly in the back of my head. I watched as Dex slowly slunk back up my body so gracefully, his cat making himself known in his movements.

He bent his head and kissed me long and deep, taking in my panting breaths. His hands on my hips he flipped me over onto my knees. I expected him to enter me hard and fast, but instead he pushed in slowly taking his time, loving me with gentle strokes. Just as I thought I would scream from the need to come again, he lifted me and wrapped his arms tightly around my chest, under my breasts. Nuzzling my hair out of the way, he started licking my mating scar. My pussy started to pulse in time with each lick, he was rocking into me harder and harder. I felt the pierce of his teeth as they re-marked me and I came, sobbing in my mate's arms as he flooded me with his cum.

After a while, I became aware of him slowly and gently moving in and out of me, lapping gently at my mating mark. His hand cupped my jaw, turning his head towards me. His lips found mine, kissing me gently, then moving slowly over my cheeks. I felt gentle kisses on my eyelids and finally he stopped, with his lips pressed firmly on my forehead.

Inside me, he was getting hard again and I whimpered with need. Lifting me off him, he turned me onto my back. He pushed pillows under my hips, lifting me higher. Pushing back into me, he rocked us gently, his eyes never leaving mine. His eyes filled with love and I felt his hands gently cup my still flat stomach.

I put my hands over his, joining our fingers together and watched as he tilted his head back and pumped into me faster and faster, coming with a roar.

He came down over me caging me in his arms and nuzzling into my neck, breathing in our joint scent deeply. I wrapped my arms and legs tightly around him and just held onto this moment.

He slowly drew away as if reluctant to leave me. "Shower or bath?" he asked.

I gave a huge yawn "Shower," I said, as my stomach rumbled, "and food!" I smiled.

He picked me up and took me into our bathroom, setting me on the ledge in the shower while he got the water going.

We washed each other gently, taking the time to just be. This was just what we needed after the stress of the last few days.

Drying us, Dex got me into bed then wrapped a towel around his hips and went to get us something to eat.

He came back about ten minutes later with milk, sandwiches and biscuits. We made quick work of devouring our midnight feast.

A little later, feeling sufficiently full, we snuggled down, listening to the rain that had started coming down and enjoying the cool breeze coming through the open door.

As I drifted off to sleep in the comfort of my mate's arms, I reflected that even with all that had occurred over the last few days, they had been good days. Meeting Annie and her boys had been the icing on the cake, although it had made me miss my sisters more.

The Catch-Up

It had been a couple of weeks since the poachers had hit the Whytes' farm. My belly was starting to show, and I was now sporting a small baby bump. As a wolf, I would be pregnant for approximately six months. I wasn't sure if I was happy about this or not. At least the nine months humans got gave them more time to prepare.

I had let my sisters know and they were thrilled. They were all going to try and come out to see us, either before the birth or after. I was hoping that by next Christmas, they would have all been, although I had a feeling that Jaq was going to come out earlier.

When I had last spoken to her, she was restless. She had been out of the military for about six months and was struggling to settle down. She had been travelling all over the USA, trying to decide what she wanted to do and picking up flying jobs as and when she could. I knew that next week she would be checking in with April in our hometown to see how she and our little sisters were doing. I would see if I could get a better read on her then.

But today we were on our way to the monthly meeting of the families and this time the Whytes' were coming. This would be the first meeting since the poachers had hit them. I knew that the knowledge they had would be important, improving the lives of all on the properties.

Lottie was out of the hospital, but she hadn't returned to the Moores' farm. Much to Renee's dismay. She had asked for all her stuff to be packed up and sent to the Whytes' while she was still in the hospital. Stating that she wouldn't be stepping a foot back on to that land, while her father's name was still on the deeds, because she didn't want to chance running it to him. Her sisters had been told they could visit her whenever they wanted at the Whytes' farm.

On leaving the hospital she moved straight in with Kyle, Annie. She was doing much better, but still suffered from dizziness, it was a good reminder that even though shifters were tough, we could still be hurt.

Amy was moving between homes, much to Joel's discomfort. He was thrilled that his sister had had found her mates, but as wild dogs lived in family packs, he was struggling. Their parents had decided to retire to the coast now that their children were grown and had turned everything over to Joel and Amy, as their other children weren't interested in farming at all and most had moved out of the country.

Amy was moving between Annie's home and her childhood home, so that she could still help her brother out. I knew part of today's meeting would be to sort out housing, so that Joel wasn't so stressed.

I was looking forward to seeing everyone and catching up. I had brought along the feedback forms for Annie's various jams and sauces and unsurprisingly, it was all positive. Maggie couldn't wait to get more from her, so I'd also brought an order with me.

Pulling in under the trees after a fairly uneventful ride, I was surprised to see almost everyone was there already. It looked like we were only waiting on Kyle and Lottie.

My door opened and Dex was there to lift me out, even though I was more than capable. I knew his leopard was in a majorly protective mode, so I let him pamper me as much as I could handle. We'd argued last week about my working, even though I was already only handling the small animals. Eventually, I had appealed to Jett to please speak to him.

I moved out from under his arms straight into Annie's and was given a big hug. There was much happiness on all the females' faces, as they took in my small bump.

Hearing another vehicle arriving we turned to see Lottie and Kyle. Her hair was still short where it had been shaved for the operation relieve the pressure in her head, but on the whole, she looked well. Her face broke into a smile when she saw her sisters. As she went to open her door, I saw Kyle say something to her. She pulled a face and frowned at him. He just laughed at her, then got out and made his way round to help her out.

Pulling her gently out of the vehicle like she was made of spun glass, he helped her down. His arm around her shoulders as they walked over to us. Her sisters were fairly vibrating, with the need to get to their sister.

"Kyle!" I heard Annie say in a firm voice.

He sighed and rolled his eyes at his mother.

"I know." He muttered removing his arm from Lottie's shoulder and let her go. She was quickly surrounded by her sisters, who were laughing and crying at the same time. Kyle came over to us and dropped a kiss on his mother's cheek. Then went around all the males, greeting everyone with chin lifts or manly backslapping hugs, depending on the male.

After Lottie was released by her sisters Amy and I finally got our hugs in.

Her eyes went down to my belly and welled with tears. I noticed Kyle coming towards us, but she stopped him with raised hand. "Happy tears, babe, happy tears." Hugging me tight she whispered, "I'm so happy for you both."

Entwining my arm with hers I grinned. "You're welcome to go and congratulate him, if your mate will let you, that is."

She laughed and called out, "Babe, I'm just letting you know I'm hugging Dex."

Kyle growled at her, but my mate didn't seem to be bothered, as he hugged one of his oldest friends. They spent a bit of time talking softly to each other before Zane pushed in.

"Stop hugging the little sister, Dex, sharing is caring, you know. It's my turn. Loving the shorn look, Lotts. Looking hot, babe," he grinned at her.

Laughing as she punched his arm, Lottie was passed around everyone. Much to Kyle's disgust, even his brothers got in on hugging her, which made all of us laugh.

Eventually, he'd enough and pulled her away, down onto his lap where he sat at the table, grumbling under his breath.

Lottie just laughed and gave him a sweet kiss which calmed his alpha ass down considerably.

Finally, Dex called the meeting to order. After Amy and Zane went through the finances, the Whytes' were given an explanation all the businesses and how they worked.

I updated Annie on our thoughts about her jams and sauces. Dex suggested she should consider going into business and selling from a shop in town. She was interested but wanted to see more information first. I knew that Dex's family had an empty storefront that he was thinking of. They decided to each put up a proposal and decide at the next meeting.

Housing for Amy, Rory and Sean was decided. They opted to combine finances and build a brand-new house between the Landry property and the Whytes'. They'd have their privacy, but the distance would only be twenty minutes by vehicle from house to house.

Joel looked relieved while Amy was ecstatic.

The talk then turned to transport and getting people out quickly in the case of emergencies. It was agreed that having a plane at the disposal of all the families would be better and more cost-effective in the long run. Jett had told us at breakfast the day after we had all got back that John, their go-to pilot, was retiring as he had failed his most recent eyesight test.

Rory and Sean looked at each other "You could have a helicopter as well as a plane, just in case. If there's enough money."

Anton looked interested "We would then need pilots," he said.

"Both Rory and I can fly, but we'll need to renew our licences."

"I may have a solution to a pilot for planes or helicopters," I said.

They all looked at me.

"My sister' been out of the military for six months and is struggling to settle."

Rory and Sean both nodded at me, seeming to know what I meant. I saw Amy lay a hand on each of them.

"She's visiting our other sister April next week and I can speak to her then. She's a trained military pilot in both helicopters and planes, but she's been flying small planes since she was sixteen, well, twelve actually.   I think if she's agreeable she'd be a great fit."

"What exactly do you mean when you say she's been flying since she was twelve?" asked Anton.

I grinned happily around the table. "Jaq is an Eagle Shifter, so a career as a pilot was perfect for her."

"Wait," said Sean. "You don't mean Jaqueline Channing, do you?"

"Yes, she's, my sister."

Sean and Rory looked at each other then, at Dex.

"You want her, Dex. She was the best pilot we had in our unit."

By now I was fairly bouncing in my seat with excitement.

"You know my sister!"

They both nodded looking amused at my excitement.

"Awesome. So, can I ask her next week?" I looked around at the rest of the table who all seemed to be amused by me.

"Go ahead and ask her, love," agreed Dex.

I was beside myself. I couldn't wait to speak to Jaq next week. This week was going to go by so slowly.

The meeting finished after that, so we all went to the vehicles and got the good we had brought with out of the cool boxes. We sat under the trees taking time to catch up and see how the new mating's' were going.

It was lovely just to spend time soaking in the comfort of being with family.

Epilogue

We were sitting at the table after just eating dinner, catching up on the day's happenings on the ranch, the vet service and the clinic.

It had been a busy couple of months. I looked around the table at my brothers chatting. Even Duke was looking amused at something Zane was telling them. Falcon had moved his mate from her chair and onto his lap and was listening with an amused grin on his face, his other hand running through his mate's hair.

Looking to my right, I noticed my beautiful Reggie watching them all with bright happy eyes, although those eyes seemed to be a bit strained around the edges at the moment. She was leaned back in her chair as far as was comfortable for her, which, at this late stage in her pregnancy wasn't very comfortable. She never complained though no matter how uncomfortable or tired she got.

I'd been taking her out to the swimming pool every night for the last month of her pregnancy, to just float in the water to give her body some relief. It was Annie who suggested it to me and I was so grateful to her.

I watched as a ripple went over her stomach and caught her flinching and closing her eyes. Putting my hand over her bump I checked my watch and waited for the next one. It came exactly five minutes later.

Catching Jett's eye, I showed him five with my hand. He nodded and came over to Reggie and squatted down.

"Hey little mama, how long have you been in labour?"

She sighed looking at me from the corner of her eye.

"About five hours. My water hasn't broken yet though."

I knew she had kept quiet about being in labour because she didn't want me to worry about her. What she didn't realise yet was that I worried anyway.

Picking her up, I walked straight out of the dining room, shouting over my shoulder.

"We'll meet you at the clinic."

I heard them all start talking over each other as we left them behind.

I knew we needed this time together before our babies got here. We'd found out two months ago that we were expecting twins, although we hadn't found out what we were having exactly, much to the dismay of our family and friends. I knew there was a bet going on about whether they would be male or female young.

Resting her head on my shoulder she slanted her eyes up at me.

"I love you so much, my love. It was the best decision I ever made taking the job as a vet here. I can't wait to meet our little ones."

I pressed a kiss to her temple, breathing her in.

"You complete me, Reggie. I didn't realise how lost and lonely I was until you came into my life. I can't wait to see what other adventures await us."

Two hours after leaving the dining room we welcomed the next line of MacGregors into the world.

I kissed my mate's head looking proudly down at our beautiful babies. Both boys, with my red hair and their mother's eyes.

The End

Acknowledgements

I would like to say a massive thank you to my fellow author and friend Cloe Rowe. Without your encouragement and help this book would never have seen the light of day. One of the best things I have ever done was contact you after reading your first book Redemption Ranch. You have been an inspiration from day one.

To the lovely Jeneveir Evans our early morning chats (well early for me, late nights for you) and suggestions have been invaluable. Thank you for taking the time from your busy schedule to help me. Keep that saga going!

My eldest daughter Helen who every day offered positive quotes and comments during this journey. I love you more than the whole world and don't know what I would do without you and your encouragement. Thank you for my beautiful book covers and making me a font just for me. Love you, baby.

To my husband for always encouraging me on whatever crazy idea takes me at the time. Being there for me, for treating me like a queen. You are my inspiration.

I want to say a massive THANK YOU!

To all those who read my first unedited version of this book. For taking a chance on a new author and for reaching out with positive comments and suggestions. Without you the next book featuring Lottie and Kyle would never have been started.

So, from the bottom of my heart thank you.

About the Author

I grew up on a cattle farm on the outskirts of a small town in Zambia, which is in Southern Central Africa. I went to school in South Africa, Zambia and finally finished my schooling in Zimbabwe. I had an amazing childhood filled with fantastic experiences. As a family, we often holidayed at Lake Kariba and I feel very privileged to have seen Victoria Falls, one of the seven wonders of the world several times.

My grandparents lived on the same farm as my parents and me. It was my grandmother, my Ouma who first introduced me to the romance genre and I was hooked from there.

I now live happily in Jane Austen country in the UK with family.

Follow me:

Email: michelledups@yahoo.com

https://www.facebook.com/michelle.dups.5/

https://www.instagram.com/michelle-s_belle_s

www.michelledups.carrd.co

THANK YOU!

Thank you for taking the time and a chance on me, I hope you enjoy reading my books as much as I enjoy writing them. Books make life a little easier to handle in these strange times.

I write what I like to read, and life is hard enough as it is, so there is little angst in my books. They all have a have a happy ending, a strong family vibe with strong alpha males and strong females.

The reason I wrote this book was that the last year hasn't been the best for anyone really and I decided that I wanted to start knocking things off my bucket list. As travel was off the cards .... I decided with much encouragement from fellow authors and my family to dust off my notes from the book I started in 1999 while still living in Africa.

I know you will have lots of questions after this book, but some of this will be answered in Kyle and Lottie's book –

ANGEL. You will find out why her father hates her so much. You will also get to meet some new characters in this book.

I hope you have enjoyed reading about Dex and Reggie and the MacGregor family and friends.

I love to hear from my readers so please feel free to message me on any of my social media.

If I could be so cheeky as to ask you to please leave a review, these are truly helpful to indie authors.

Much love to all my readers.

NEXT BOOK IN SERIES

Sanctuary Book 2 - ANGEL (Kyle and Lottie's story)

EXCERPTS FROM REVIEWS FOR WILD & FREE ON AMAZON & GOODREADS

AMAZON

COULDN'T PUT IT DOWN

The characters catch you straight away, can't wait for more in the series, was totally immersed.

GREAT NEW SHIFTER SERIES

I'm completely intrigued by this new series.

GOODREADS

GREAT READ

Really enjoyed this debut book by this author. The story was great and the characters were awesome.